MAKING CONNECTIONS

by

JANN KING

Five Unusual Stories

Published by New Generation Publishing in 2015

Copyright © Jann King 2015

First Edition

The author asserts the moral right under the Copyright, Designs and Patents Act 1988 to be identified as the author of this work.

All Rights reserved. No part of this publication may be reproduced, stored in a retrieval system or transmitted, in any form or by any means without the prior consent of the author, nor be otherwise circulated in any form of binding or cover other than that which it is published and without a similar condition being imposed on the subsequent purchaser.

www.newgeneration-publishing.com

New Generation Publishing

TABLE OF CONTENTS

FAT LADY'S SONGS 1

BRIGHTON INCIDENTAL 28

CROSSING LINES 46

MADELEINE TIME 76

FINN 84

FAT LADY'S SONGS

"It's a button pick! Large buttons, everybody!"

Hell! Snipping all those little stalks! Grading! Couldn't do ten baskets an hour now. Fiddling about with damn little piddling mushrooms! All thumbs and pesky rubber gloves! The old man scratched his nose with one truculent finger and dumped his bucket, and rack filled with boxes, by the wall at the far end of the row. He was also at the far end of the shed. There was less and less light, like a tunnel. "Bloody moles!"

He stood in a space barely two feet wide, perhaps twenty feet long. Above him on either side reared stacks of wooden trestles like dining tables with sawed down legs, piled on top of each other to a height of perhaps eleven feet. Mushrooms swarmed over every one of them:--the buttons, clumped like arthritic fists, the big ones, huddled in their coolie hats, and the smooth, white, "best" cups that reminded him of smug little nuns.

Twenty-four trestles to a row. Thirty rows to a shed. "Stalag bloody mushroom!"

Radio One blared out suddenly, further up the shed. ". . . of Sutton Coldfield! And . . here's a wacky one for you!," the DJ's voice effused in triumph. "Somebody's offering a vasectomy as a raffle prize, folks! Can you believe that? Worth all of three hundred pounds. Well, better than a bouncing seven and a half, I'd say! Keep the calls coming. Aaaand . . ." his voice dropped cosily, "stay on the . . er . . ball!" He chortled. "Don't go away now! And as I . . . er . . . *peter* out . . ." Music thrummed up. "Any more wacky stories and we want to know." The beat pounded. "Back soon." A splatter of drums finally knocked him into oblivion.

The old man ground his teeth and spat in the direction of a crushed bit of mushroom on the concrete floor. "Missed!" He clambered his way up to the top trestle, his feet braced evenly between the two rows pot-holer fashion, hooked his bucket and his boxes' rack over the side of the upper bed, and sneezed. "Bloody spores!" He picked up his knife and reached for a cluster of buttons. Stalks pelted into the bucket, mushrooms lobbed into a box with the casual ease of habit.

Two women in neighbouring rows, unable to see each other, discussed Doris's husband, "mean devil!" who'd just cleared off with Josie Potter, "nothing but a tart," and left two kids and a baby on his wife's hands.

"Pity 'e didn't 'ave a vasectomy! I know what I'd like to do if I was Doris!" She brandished the knife. "What?" said her companion, unable to see the gesture. Her tone, however, suggested prurient anticipation. The old man heard muttering, followed by triumphant laughter.

On his other side, a fifteen-year-old youth, off from school for the holidays, discussed the latest Test Match debacle with a similarly invisible companion. The adolescent voices had a harsh edge, a tone that lacked modulation, suggesting an as yet unaccustomed masculinity, like tight new shoes. Their words raced with fervour, shot up the scale, erupted in guffaws, or mimicked the radio beat.

One of the women climbed to the top trestle, her bucket clanking, and came abruptly face to face with the old man. Her plain, maternal face smiled good-naturedly. He glared at her in silence. "All right, are you?" Her tone coaxed at him as if he were a recalcitrant child. Still he said nothing. She smiled at him, undaunted. "Where you livin' now, Al?"

He grabbed at a clump of mushrooms. "Cemetery!"

That would shut her up. Nosey old biddy!

"Oh well, that's all right, then." She continued to smile, unperturbed, and bent to her half of the mushroom bed.

Yet he had spoken no less than the truth. "Always puts 'em off the scent!" He was dossing out in an uncultivated corner of a cemetery. Custodians and vicars often turned a blind eye. He'd be all right for a while, if he didn't catch the attention of some sanctimonious windbag or wittering lady councillor. In any case, he left at sunrise to get a couple of hours in on his Project before turning up at the mushroom farm at 8:00 a.m. "Can't finish Projects without dosh. Need caboodle!"

Al liked cemeteries. They were cities he knew and understood. He had made the acquaintance of hundreds of their inhabitants over the years. They were, of course, too polite to bother him unless he sought them out; and he had plenty of choice. Somehow they made him feel one up. Definitively one up! Which is more than you could say in Bristol or Derby. For in the midst of the great democracy of the dead, his own pumping heart and gusting breath seemed to confer upon him the sceptre of royalty. Only his Projects, of course, could confer a crown.

Now take this graveyard here. Under the birches in the Eastern corner, by a comfortable old wall, lay Jenny Postlethwaite: 'Born May 20, 1817; Received into the Heavenly Kingdom February 5, 1841'. Consumption, probably, or the arrival of her fifth child. It didn't say 'Beloved wife of . . .', so he had to guess. "Hello, Jen. How's it going? A bit blowy today."

Then there was Sarah and Joseph Hamilton. In fact, there were two Joseph Hamiltons, and Jonathan, Emilia and Phoebe as well. The family sarcophagus, dauntingly large and white, dominated the cemetery as they had no doubt dominated the community in life. A black chain fence flounced gracefully around it, paralleled by a rosy slab path, separating it from the vulgar encroachment of other people's daisies. An angel, frozen in unctuous gesture, bestowed Everlasting Love upon their heads.

"No time to bother with you today, Joseph One. I'm off to have a gab with Jenny, and Francis Higson next door. Poor old Higson. 'Scholar.' That's all it said. Died at forty. Al spat. "Don't we bloody all!" He cleared his throat as unsettling memories stirred. The grave was shabby, apologetic. "Head in the clouds, died a pauper, no doubt about that."

Then there was Gilbert Ernest Simpkin, who had 'Passed on without an Angel's warning', aged 20, in 1932. Motorcycle accident, probably. 'Pray For Me', said the headstone, a smooth granite affair. "Said one for yer today, Gil." He stopped and scratched his head, "'Course, it could have been a drowning."

He would potter back and forth, arranging his newspapers, his enamel mug, his tins of sardines. Occasionally he would pat a large, lidded mushroom basket affectionately. Two placid frogs had inhabited it for a fortnight. He exercised the little creatures several times a day on a generous length of twine secured at the ankle. He would release them, just like all the others, in a week or so, or whenever he moved on. Whichever came first. There was sure to be a stray cat further on, or a pigeon, or even a mouse.

Dogs you couldn't abandon. So the old man never sought them out, though he shared many a meal with an inquisitive mutt. But never more than one meal. "Can't have you tagging along, old fella. What you need is vittels and a fireside, not an old codger like me."

Still, there was a marble effigy of a little dog in this particular cemetery, sitting proudly at the headstone of an eighty-year-old woman named Lucy May Henderson. It gave him a wistful sensation whenever he passed.

Al flourished a bottle defiantly, as he rounded the end of the Hamilton extravaganza. "Up yours, Joseph, old son!" He cackled genially. "'Ow's yer father?"

The habit of insult, however, was not confined to puncturing the supposed vanity of phantoms. It had proved a disconcerting attention-getter among the living. For one thing, he deplored women with immense bottoms, who always seemed to be stuffing their faces with ice cream or chips. "It's . . . it's . . . unaesthetic!" He rolled the word around his mouth like a choice wine. He approached, glared. "Don't you think you've eaten enough of those already, for God's sake, woman?"

She gazed at him in bovine amazement, a chip halfway to her mouth. "What?" Her features re-formed in an expression of wild-eyed outrage. "Mind your own business, you cheeky old devil!"

"In that case," his gravelly voice rose to take in any immediate passers-by, "I just wonder how many lavatory seats you must have broke, that's what I wonder!" He spat for effect. "When you can get your arse through the door, that is!" And off he would shamble, leaving the hapless victim crimson with embarrassment, surrounded by the usual gaping bystanders.

If he met a screaming child having a tantrum in the street, he would approach at once and bawl in its face: "Shut up, you little brat!" leaving the child open-mouthed with astonishment—and silent—and the mother white with anger. Probably, he thought in the final analysis, because he had achieved what she couldn't!

Beer bellies revolted him. He would saunter purposefully up to his target and wait until the man returned his gaze. "Must be years since you've seen it, mate!"

A startled pause. Narrowed eyes. "What?"

"What, he says! God, it's been so long, he's forgotten to look for it! You look bloody disgusting, man. Why don't you do something about it?"

Al had discovered that it was best to be quick on his feet after this sort of sally. He had found himself in a brawl after only his second attempt to tilt at this particular windmill.

He wondered if it did any good. He supposed not. But you never knew. Anyhow, it was a kind of revenge.

Another fulfilling moment came whenever he caught sight of a parked sports car. The driver always seemed to be an alarmingly vigorous young man with gelled hair and a tan.

"Jumped up little pricks!" He would choose his moment, sidle up to the car, glance around surreptitiously, then give the bloody thing a good bash with his foot.

Passers-by would see a sunburned old chap crabbing his way down the street in some haste, cackling with delight and slapping his thigh. Occasionally limping. More often than not, he would be clutching a large, cloudy bottle. A casual observer might have assumed it to be some evil mix. Vodka, perhaps. But it was only barley water. "Keeps me ticking over nicely."

He also hated solicitors, rice ('Burma Road'), litter, banks, telephone kiosks, mobile phones (antisocial twerps), horses ('all nose and bum'), football, ferrets, bananas . . .The list went on. In fact, it was part of Al's philosophy, indeed one of his proverbs, that 'Life is knowing what you don't want!' He felt it could give a sense of purpose to a lot of lives.

Not that his own was aimless. Not in the least. But there were plenty of poor sods out there who didn't know what the hell they wanted. Only that they weren't happy. If you could start by finding out what you didn't want, sometimes you found out what you did. That's how it had happened for him. And now he had his special work. His Projects.

He beamed a broken-toothed grin of satisfaction at the thought. The current Project was almost complete. As soon as this bloody mushroom pick was over at half three, he'd be off and beavering at it until sunset.

He built towers. It was a consuming passion. It was a calling. They were unique, rising twenty feet into the air, miniature Towers of Babel, modern ziggurats, suggesting both a sculpture and a 'folly';

eluding classification. He never used scaffolding. Ledges and platforms were an integral part of the construction, so that he could build ever inwards and upwards.

He had been anxious about Britain. But he'd managed two towers so far, nonetheless. One on a remote escarpment of Dartmoor; the other rearing primevally on a lonely Scottish isle. You couldn't have people standing around gawping, asking daft questions. They could gawp all they liked after it was finished and he'd sodded off. But one whiff of curiosity and he skedaddled, toute bloody suite.

He'd sleep well tonight, knowing the final touches were in sight. An absolutely bloody blissful, silent sleep, with the wholehearted approval of his quiet companions under the stars. No need of the Salvation Army yet. Not in this weather. In fact—he cackled to himself—he'd sleep the sleep of the dead. Nobody to find fault. Nobody nagging. He shivered involuntarily, as an old, relentless fist began to pummel at the gates of memory.

It had been decades. But he could still feel his soul diminish like a sponge clenched dry at the sound of her remembered voice. It wrenched at your entrails. It droned. It clawed you into tatters. It sucked your lifeblood like a vampire, until even the will to live had dwindled to a barely flickering spark. But she never seemed to grasp the destruction.

He'd tried to be a good husband. 'I, Allardice James Anthony, take thee, Alice Joanna. That was in '58, and he had started on the railway the same year. He was content. So was Alice, at first. Then Theresa arrived, his little Tera. Alice had turned out to be a good mother. The local station was peaceful, easy-going. It had a picket fence, and flower beds bursting with geraniums, and sweet peas and gillyflowers.

His eyelids flickered, felt damp. Those scents still had him clawing backward, longingly, into the swirling reaches of the long ago. You could say what you liked about British Rail, but he had loved the railway. The line was derelict now. The old station house had probably been turned into a public toilet, or knocked down to build a bloody concrete chip shop. "Bah!" He spat viciously. The Prince of Wales had got that right. He'd seen that in all the papers.

In fact, the old man possessed an extraordinary range of information. He had collected and rummaged through newspapers for years; especially in winter, when he hoarded them against the cold. He dipped into 'The Church Times', 'The Guardian', 'The Mirror', 'The Sun', 'The Sunday Times', 'The Independent'; even the local papers that he swapped with others of the wandering fraternity. He knew about the farming problems in Fenny Upton, and the uproar at a parish council meeting in Penbrook-under-Edge when somebody heaved a prayer book at the vicar. He knew about Salman Rushdie, the death of Michael Jackson, ex-President Clinton's misdemeanours, ObamaCare, the Oscars, Beckham and Posh, Angelina and Brad, the rise of UKIP, the Yew Tree investigations. He was familiar with avian flu, Big Brother, tsunamis, and Taylor Swift's love life. He had read amusing facts about Halifax Town Hall. He had a hazy idea about deforestation in Brazil. And if he got it wrong, well, Jenny Postlethwaite wouldn't mind; and Francis Higson, 'scholar', would be too polite to comment.

Which is more than you could say for Alice. He supposed he must have simply been inadequate for what she wanted. Or thought she wanted.

"Well somebody's got to tell you a few home truths, Al!"

He tried to wipe the perspiration from his forehead, remembered he was wearing rubber gloves, cursed, and wiped his face on his sleeve. The radio throbbed. Somehow, the repetitive beat sounded exactly like her nagging.

"You're not . . . and what's more, you'll never . . . What makes you think you could . . . ?" The voice bludgeoned on, the intonations melodramatic with contempt. "You? You!? That'll be the day! You're just not . . . are you? Well are you? Why can't you . . ? You ought to . . . you don't . . . you shouldn't . . . you can't hold a candle to . . . Why isn't . . . ? Other men . . . You'll never amount to anything . . ."

And the worst one of all, which regularly annihilated him: "You're forgettable, Allardice, utterly forgettable!"

One Saturday he went up to the corner shop for a packet of fags and a tin of cocoa and never came back. He wrote to Tera, of course. But he became a missing person. He grew some stubble, threw away his watch, bought a strange hat, and buggered off to the furthest docks he could find. He found somebody who recommended, in whispers, the name of "this bloke who'll get you a new passport for the right price." It took him six months of grinding labour. But he got the passport and a new identity.

"Tea break everybody! Tea!"

Al came to himself with less of a start than usual from one of his reveries. Something had already tugged at the edge of his awareness before he heard the supervisor's words. Then he realised what it was. The radio had been switched off.

A seemly hush descended, as if in homage to the Fungal God. It had invaded his consciousness as the numinous peace in all good places of worship should. He stabbed his knife into the compost, clambered down, ducked under the rack filled with blue cardboard boxes, and pulled gingerly at the rubber gloves. Tricky, this. He had already learned the folly of haste, and been forced to spend three days with the tips of two glove fingers and a thumb missing. This time patience triumphed, and with a pleased grunt he flapped the pink gloves—neat, expended little udders—over the end of a trestle, ready for his return.

He was about to reach for his bucket when he paused, his eyes dancing. A smirk appeared. One pink rubber finger, defiant to the end, was pointing vulgarly heavenward.

The smirk broadened into a grin. "Know what you mean!" He shook his head at the odd collusion of objects in the meaning of the universe. Then, grabbing his bucket filled with stalks, he ambled out of the shed into the full glare of mid-morning. He up-ended the bucket into a green skip marked 'chocs only', dumped it on the ground, and followed the line of blue-smocked pickers over to the cafeteria hut.

On either side stretched other sheds, identically grey-roofed and green-doored. Blank, functional. His gaze swept the compound again. "Carbuncles!" he muttered. "Bloody carbuncles!"

The cafeteria, shabby and uncomfortable with its stained formica tables and tubular chairs, already droned with a dozen conversations, interspersed with the desultory clunk of tea and coffee mugs. Al picked up a full mug of tea and shambled over to the furthest table. But as usual there was no escape. He was hemmed in almost at once by a gaggle of co-workers from shed 6A.

"Tell us about the time you was a mountie in the Yukon, then, Al," tittered Madge. A scrubbed young schoolgirl with a frizzed topknot leaned forward, her mouth open. The older women, noting her earnest expression, laughed.

Al scowled. "I'll tell you this, and you can put it on your pins and knit it if you want. I went to Canada all right. Ah. I did. Worked in New Zealand on a sheep farm an' all." His eyes flickered irascibly from face to face. "Beautiful creatures, sheep. Peaceful. More bleating in here than there is out there!" He swallowed from the mug. "Went to South Africa. Went to the good old U. S. of A." His gaze seemed to hover for a moment, turn inward. "Made some dosh. Sent it to the young un."

"You had a kid, Al ?" Brenda's voice rose in amazement. She took off her glasses and rubbed them on her sleeve.

He cackled. "What do you think, I've been a monk?"

Rita nudged Phyllis. But Phyllis's face remained solemn. "Where is he n …"

"She!"

"… *she*, now then, Al?" Rita attempted a credulous smile. "In the Yukon with the mounties?"

There was a smattering of laughter.

"So she had all of it—your money—did she, then Albert?" Malcolm, a chubby economics student, spoke up for the first time. He was always interested in the money angle.

"And just what makes you think my name's Albert?"

Malcolm looked confused.

Al steepled his fingers and leaned back in his chair. "Invested my bit." He paused. "And the name is Allardice."

This created a stir, an "Oh, very posh" from Brenda, and a stammered apology from Malcolm.

"Allardice of the Yukon," giggled Phyllis.

"Well, you can't forget a name like that in a hurry," said Madge.

Like a darting fish, pain registered in the old man's eyes as, unbidden, he heard once more Alice's voice echoing back from the long ago: " . . . You're forgettable, Allardice, utterly forgettable . . ." Then it was gone.

Resuming the offensive, he leaned forwards and tapped the side of his nose conspiratorially. "Art, you might say, that's where I invested my bit." Raising his mug, he looked round at the effect on his listeners, and gulped triumphantly. The foreman, who had been leaning against the wall chewing a cigarette, laughed.

"Oh well," broke in Rita, as the general amusement subsided, "pardon us. We didn't know we was sharing a table with an investment banker!"

He reddened with outrage. "Don't you go accusing me of laying down with swine!"

Brenda stepped in hastily. "What was you looking for then with all these foreign places and everything?"

"Looking for? A fabled shore. What do you think? Daft question!"

"And did you find one?" The schoolgirl's eyes searched his face with wondering attention. The old man turned to look at her. The shading of his voice altered slightly.

"There aren't any fabled shores, little Miss Inquisitive. Except what's inside your own head."

And so it continued for a few more interminable minutes. Nobody believed a word he said, of course.

"Back to work everybody!" The foreman grinned, jabbing at his watch. Chairs scraped. Conversations fuelled into the usual grumbling. Arms rose, as last swigs were dredged from the bottom of mugs. Chocolate wrappers were crumpled, cigarette packets jammed into pockets. The exodus straggled back.

Theresa—his little Tera—she had written to him for years. In foreign places, under the coded names they invented. After she left home to take up nursing. After she qualified. And still she wrote. Meandering letters. Once in a while.

She had told him when Alice died. He was shocked at the way he took it. Even as he heard himself muttering: "Probably nagged herself to death," something inside him contracted. His face crumpled up. The sobs were rasping, male, dredged up from some forgotten cellar of the spirit. He cried for the waste. It was a bereavement for what might have been.

Tera wrote again. After a depressing involvement with the wrong kind, she had found herself a decent chap. "A good man," she said. "Good sort. Loves me to bits, Dad."

"Finally, someone who deserves you, pet. Told you he'd come along."

She got married.

About a year later, Al had been leaning on the rail of a steamer staring into the brown swirl of the Mississippi when the boat listed violently and swung round. In minutes, it went down. He could still remember the screaming, and the viciously wrenching water. It was muddy, and horrifyingly warm.

Five bodies hadn't been found. It was assumed they had been swept down into the Gulf of Mexico. One description—a man unidentified at the time—uncannily matched his own. And so it was that Fate offered him the answer to the hankering in his heart.

He got a buddy, an itinerant fruit picker, to send a dictated note. He could still remember folding it and sliding it into the envelope with the newspaper clipping. He remembered the shadows of eucalyptus leaves nodding over his arm. He remembered hot coals in his throat as the cheap brown rectangle left his hand. "Better this way. You'll forget me, anyway. No good to you now, love. No point anymore." He thought of a pink-cheeked little girl sitting on his knee. "You'll be all right."

And so he let her go. With pain. With longing. With resolve. Only an old black and white snapshot bound them together now, creased, yellowing, but always smiling. He sewed it into his hatband.

Something rang sharply against the concrete floor. Shit, he'd dropped his knife. He wiped his face on his sleeve, clambered down and retrieved it. The radio blared. The day dragged inexorably forward. The lunch break came and went.

"That's my row!" It was Perce Mason—retired, self-absorbed, and querulous. They'd only been back in the shed a few moments.

"No it's not!"

"'T is! Those are my mushrooms!"

"Oh, have 'em and be buggered!" Al stomped a few yards further down the shed, then spun round, quick on the draw, and lobbed a rotten mushroom over the trestles on to what he hoped was the old fool's head.

"Who are you calling an old fool?" shouted Perce. "You're older 'n me!"

Al spat loudly. "You can't even pee straight!" A fistful of best buttons came raining over the trestles in Al's direction, and splatted on the floor several feet short of the target. He cackled contemptuously. "Missed!" He paused for effect. "Again!"

He was saluting the hidden Perce with the traditional two fingers as Elaine, the supervisor, came bustling up, her mouth twitching, to cajole him further down the shed. He raised a mushroom in defiance, brandished it at her, and ate it.

Reluctantly, he settled down once more to the disjointed rhythms of the pick. "Sod this!" He'd never make the bonus target at this rate. He decided to accelerate. His hand darted for a clump of buttons in the middle of the bed. In his haste, he knocked over some big ones near the front. They lay there accusingly, stalks up-ended. He cursed and grabbed at them savagely. A few, blotched with disease, found their way into a healthy basket. He felt like spitting. No time to muck about weeding them out now! He hoped nobody would notice.

He thrust his shoulders further over the bed, his head brushing the trestle above. "Bunks in steerage!"

His fingers closed on a young button, and it broke in half under the pressure of his thumb. Minutes later, a perfect best cup, that he hadn't intended to pick at all, came off its stalk, flew from his fingers and smashed on the floor below.

He ground his teeth. It brought forcibly to mind another of his philosophies, a new proverb he had come up with since he had been working at the mushroom farm: 'The Almighty is a pretty damn careless mushroom picker as well!'

He slowed down. Again, his mind drifted.

He'd eked out a living, drifting. Sometimes he'd made money. Sometimes. Other times . .

"You are charged with vagrancy under the law of . . ."

He had grown increasingly uncommunicative. But slowly, mysteriously, an unfocussed yearning to make something, build something, had come upon him. He almost thought of it as a twisted yearning for the loss of his child. His spirit reached out, but did not know where to go. He did not recognise in himself the slow unfolding of a long suppressed creative nature, slumbering like a bulb under winter earth. But he did know that he lacked the means to express whatever the hell it was that was bugging him. It was like wanting to draw when you didn't have a pencil.

There had been women. At first he thought that must be it—wanting them. Or wanting to be part of a couple, perhaps. Then, one May night, he'd been in New Orleans with a woman, a very pretty woman. They had strolled through the French quarter, fingers loosely entwined, gazing through the lacy, wrought iron gates into secret and abundant gardens tumescent with fragrance, overflowing with juniper and jasmine, with clamouring tuberoses and lolling blossoms that suggested indolence and desire.

"Close your eyes," he said softly. "Take a deep breath." She obeyed.

The garden wrapped its exotic miasma around them like a cloak. Somewhere nearby, jazz poured from a hidden doorway into a night pristine and starred. Leaves rustled gently. Languid Spanish moss trailed from the boughs of a tree. A fountain glimmered under a waning moon, and somewhere a bird poured out cadences of sweetness in counterpoint to a distant saxophone.

"What do you smell?" He looked up at the bright constellations, absorbed, aroused, waiting.

"Cat pee", she said.

He'd given up on women after that. And he had come at last to his Projects. This Project, here in a highly populated county, had been a challenge. He had wanted to know whether it could be done, whether, in fact, a site could be found. Farmers had seemed the best bet. He hadn't realised the word 'No' could carry so many inflections. One farmer had added: "Bugger off or I'll set the dogs on you, you old nutter!"

But at last, somebody had felt intrigued enough to give the old chap a hearing, and desperate enough about the pile of rubbish behind the barn. "You clear it, you can have the space. No use to me. But don't ask for money! No dossing! No pals! And don't bring any booze!"

Of such stuff are the patrons of Art.

He had bought the usual equipment: oxyacetylene torch, gas cylinders, goggles, cables, a drill, paint, scrap metal, rivets, chisels, saws, files, slabs, sea shells, marbles, gloves, hammers, plaster, clay, pliers, and so forth—all with the wages he had hoarded from his labours at the mushroom farm.

This one was his fourteenth tower. He chuckled. His mind cast back once more to Louisiana. Not New Orleans—he spat in disgust—but to a place near Lake Pontchartrain. That's where, hesitant and driven, he'd built the first one. And all because an old black woman in a yellow dress had mucked about with a pack of tarot cards.

She had reeked of pork fat and greens. "Aint you got no home, honky Joe? Where you goin'?"

He had buried his head in his hands. "End of the line."

"That aint too smart. Hey, maybe you'll get yoursel' a break!" She moved closer. "You wanna know? Ah can tell it."

He saw again the resigned, grief-stained face with its yellowed eyes, the exhausted breasts, the drooping shoulders of a human soul without hope. "Goin' to mah grave soon." She shrugged. "It don't bother me none."

She shook him with a surprisingly strong grip. "Don't you got no sense, huh? Look. Right here. I got cards. Shuffle 'em up, but good."

He did so.

"This here is you, see. You's The Magician. You invents yoursel'". She peered at him searchingly.

Something flickered in his brain. Something echoed somewhere.

"I . . . I what?"

"You invents yoursel'. Creates yoursel'. That's what it say here."

The heat beat down like a mallet. Grasses wavered in the haze. He gazed at her, shook his head. "Too late now."

She smiled tiredly. "Sure is. Fer me. Ain' over for you yet, though. You make yoursel' what you want. You's The Magician!" A blue heron soared on the lake. "It aint over til the fat lady sings!"

"What?"

She spoke slowly, as if he were a child. "Aint no result til they adds up the votes. It's the show. You know. It aint over. Til the fat lady sings. That's when you adds up the score."

He had signed his Louisiana tower 'Fat Lady' when it was finally completed the following year. But she was dead by then, the woman. "I said one for yer, gel."

His thoughts were invaded by the strident voice of Elaine. "Pack up, everybody! Three thirty! Pack up!"

Half an hour later, he was back at the site of the new tower, his labours self-directed and singing in his mind, The Magician once more. The two frogs dozed under a flowerpot. Colin, the farmer's collie, sauntered about importantly, sensing a companionable equality.

Al shambled forward, clambered up a few feet, and hammered at a protruding nail. He grunted with distaste. How could he have missed seeing that until now? He gave it an extra wallop for good measure. Back on the ground again, he pushed his hat off his forehead and stepped sideways, hands at the small of his back, looking up at his handiwork.

It was twisted, lyrical, metallic, hard; it was elegant, crude, and fragile; it was ductile, embellished, phallic, enveloping. It was whimsical, brave. It had a fierce beauty. It was, in short, a statement of every possibility of the human spirit. It seemed to point like an accusing finger, obscenely, perhaps, at an all too impassive sky.

The collie snuffled at his shoes. "What do you think then, Colin?" The dog pricked its ears. It sidled over and licked his hand. Then it meandered over to the tower, sniffing, and lifted its leg.

"Ah. That's all very well. But you haven't been written up as an . . . an 'enigma', in the New York Times, have you, fella?' He still had the article. It was folded up very small in the place of honour in his hat, next to the old, smiling snapshot.

The press picture showed his two towers in Arizona and New Mexico. 'WHO? WHAT? WHY?' read the caption. The journalist had tied himself in intellectual knots with his 'strands of Creation', 'mystic symbols', 'resonances of the ineffable', and 'disparate sexuality of the universe'. Al chuckled. He wondered what that same bloke had said when they had discovered the one near Johannesburg. He smiled gently. He had signed the tower simply 'For Theresa'. He patted the dog. They'd probably bring Mother Theresa into it. He tickled its ears. The dog closed its eyes in ecstasy.

Al struck a pose. "I am a New Druid," he announced. "I am drifting the world constructing riddles." He tugged his hat forward. "So they tell me."

The dog scratched, and began an investigation of its nether regions.

The old man sat down in the shade of the barn. "I am—what was it? Oh yes, 'baffling' and . . . and 'arbitrary'. Wonder what they made of the one in the Australian outback?" He chortled. "I'm giving 'em a right bloody run for their money!"

The tower that reared in splendid isolation in Alaska said merely: 'Nexus'. The word had appealed to him. He'd got it out of an old "Reader's Digest".

He looked again at this, the fourteenth in the series. "They're all me, I s'pose." He fiddled with his collar. The dog snoozed in the sun.

Suddenly, Al remembered he had not yet looked at the papers old Charlie had dropped off last Saturday when he was passing through. He took a swig of barley water, opened the paper and settled down for a break.

It was just a small item, but his insatiable eye had caught it instantly. He stood up, heart hammering. Suddenly, he knew, against all promptings of caution, what he was going to do. He was in the same country, the same county. It couldn't hurt. Just once. The cemetery would have to slumber without him, tonight. "But first . . ." He lifted the flowerpot. The two frogs hopped away.

*   *   *

He stood in the shade of an ancient oak in a village beside a church yard gate, his hat jammed down, watching the group at the church door. His gaze was riveted on the couple in the middle. The young man struck a nonchalant pose, beaming. The girl smiled up at him and leaned over the baby cocooned in a white drift of christening lace. Al's hands clenched and unclenched. The July sun seemed unbearably bright, flashing like a new coin.

The girl turned in his direction, and something in his chest skittered like a pebble on a pond. For a moment her gaze locked with his. It registered mild curiosity. He drew back against the trunk. Her gaze passed on, flickered over a little crowd of the village curious outside the gate, and came to rest on the photographer who came bustling up the path, anxious, unctuous, and late. She listened patiently to his apologies. It was Theresa's face. Yet not Theresa's.

As if in echo to the thought, at that instant a woman of mature years strolled out of the church. She wore a pink dress and a picture hat of dusty rose chiffon. She put her hand over the crown against a sudden gust, and laughed. She was pink-cheeked, and ample, but pleasingly so. Still. A portly man with an air of quiet authority appeared behind her in the doorway, his arm around her shoulders. They looked comfortable together.

Children skipped about and had to be brought to order. Middle-aged men and a few younger ones, all in suits, stood hovering, grinning sheepishly and chaffing each other, their wives and girlfriends brilliant as the flowers in the cottage gardens opposite. The vicar made graceful gestures as he chatted. Two young girls tittered at an adolescent who turned crimson with humiliation. A few other teens were fiddling with mobile phones. Women leaned over the white bundle and cooed.

"Scrunch, everybody!" All eyes turned to the photographer. He stepped back and gestured extravagantly. "Hold him up! It's his first picture. So let's see our little scallywag's face, eh!"

The young woman laughed. Encouraged by her husband, she held the white bundle upright in front of her, hugging him like a trophy. Yards of lace fell almost to the ground.

The photographer gushed. "Is it official now, then, new little fella? Er . . little . . . er . . What . . . er . . . ?" He stopped in full flood. "What's his . . . er . . . ?" He turned hesitantly to the young husband.

"Allardice", he replied, "his name is Allardice", and smiled at his wife.

"Allardice James Anthony", she said, and smiled at the woman in the pink hat.

The old man stood stock-still. He couldn't seem to breathe. His pulse lurched, paused, then raced.

"Right", said the photographer, "a nice big smile now, young Allardice James Anthony. <u>Glow</u>, everybody!"

The camera froze them all in its everlasting summer.

He tried other angles, cajoling, congratulating. The churchyard fell silent with concentration.

In the old man's mind, too, a camera clicked, recording every changing expression, every shifting quality of the light. He blinked furiously. Second by second he could feel it slipping away, the 'now' already turning into the irrecoverable past. "Must remember it. Must!" The turn of a head, a pink shoe kicked off in the cool grass, the breeze lifting a gauzy sleeve, the pink hat swaying as she nodded in agreement when somebody leaned towards her . . . Click.

The gurgle of delight as her daughter placed the baby in her arms.

Two swallows skittered out of the shadows of the clock tower. He turned a seamed face briefly up at them. Click. The sun through leaves glistened on his damp cheek. A cat, reclining on a gravestone nearby, interrupted the washing of its paws and stared at him fixedly.

The baby began to cry. Mother and daughter leaned over it together, cooing. The girl's husband waggled his fingers and made faces. The vicar smiled blandly. A few frivolous remarks. Laughter. Ah's. Somebody was looking pointedly at a watch. With a sudden flurry, the party began to meander towards the gate. Time to celebrate elsewhere.

Al slid hastily round the tree trunk and waited. He could feel the ancient bark digging into his fingers. Dark sleeves swung by, pastel dresses, a bit of shawl, jouncing hair. The pink hat bobbed within a yard of his face. Instinctively, he reached towards it . . . and let his hand fall.

His eyes followed her until she was swallowed up in one of the cars.

He heard more laughter, saw good-natured jostling. The young husband put his hand surreptitiously on his wife's breast, and whispered something into her hair. Doors slammed. Engines revved. But louder than them all was the sound of his own thundering heart.

He gazed until the last car disappeared round a curve in the village street by The Red Lion. He seemed to be having difficulty with his throat. He blinked rapidly. An elderly woman rocked by with a Yorkshire terrier. She eyed him warily.

Slowly, he picked up the bottle of barley water, turned, and began to walk up the street in the opposite direction like a man caught in wet concrete. "One foot in front of the other. Come on, you daft old bugger!" Gritting his teeth, he plonked on.

Slowly, imperceptibly, his back began to straighten. His pace picked up until it even held a suggestion of jauntiness. Up came his chin. He shoved his hat back from his forehead, and began to chuckle. Now he was shambling past the last isolated cottages almost at a trot.

He stopped abruptly. "Here's to you, Allardice James Anthony!" He laughed aloud and hurled his bottle high in the air, letting out a roar of triumph as it smashed in the middle of the lane. He flung his arms wide. "Here's to bloody both of us!" His eyes closed for a moment as a sudden stillness enveloped him, a silent homage to the dearest things he had laid upon the altar of his heart.

His eyes flew open in a hurry as a Land Rover honked and swerved past him. Someone was mouthing curses. The old man brandished two fingers with the usual gusto. Then his eye fell on the winking shards of glass. He grinned wolfishly at the retreating vehicle's tyres.

He looked again at the ground. Hell, he'd made a proper mess! Still, "you can stuff your bottles made of plastic!" Mentally, he relegated them at once to the list that already included ferrets, big bottoms, rice, and bankers. "Now glass . . ." Diligently, he swept the broken pieces into the ditch with some leaves that reminded him of rhubarb. Only one glimmering fragment eluded him, to nestle among the clumpy hawthorn like some bizarre and indestructible droplet of champagne in the sun.

"And now, Alice gel, I've got the perfect retort for you." He stood up, smiling broadly. "Music to my ears, you might say." He spat with relish, then pirouetted in a bearish little dance along the hedgerow. "Oh yes indeedy!" He cackled and slapped his thigh.

"Forgettable am I, did you think? Well you see, Alice gel," he tugged his hat down with a gesture of finality, "it's not over til the fat lady sings! And it looks like she finally did. Today. Just for me!"

At the end of the lane, he branched off towards the road, whistling.

BRIGHTON INCIDENTAL

A good-looking man passed the window. I liked his face. He was young, his expression intent. Bowing his head against a bleak east wind, he struggled round the corner grasping the top of his coat. Yet the wind was not his prime concern. He was preoccupied. I wondered why.

I craned my neck, but the Italian restaurant window ended just where he had turned.

Now who's *that*?

I observe people. I follow them sometimes, just out of curiosity, just to discover where they're off to. If I'm really persistent I might even find out the reason. What is it about other people's lives? Do they have a pattern, or like mine, are they usually in chaos? I'd love to know. So trying to find out is a sort of hobby.

A shoal of foreign students went by like herring riding the current. A spindly teen at the back looked my way and shook his fin at me. I didn't know him, did I? Was it someone I'd followed before?

Two girls teetered by in shoes that gave the impression they were walking on ballet point, anoraks over miniskirts so skimpy there wasn't enough material to flap in the wind. An old buffer rolled past in a seaman's cap, trying to master a bag of chips. Good lord, was he leering at me?

A girl moved into my vision from the left, my attention caught by her nifty bobble hat with its pattern of Icelandic runes. Litter swirled up from the pavement but she ignored it, her head bent into the wind, her expression intent. Something about her held my gaze. Something.

I paused, a forkful of tiramisu half way to my mouth. Out of the corner of my eye, a bob-haired couple of ladies-who-lunch at the next table nudged each other, their pursed stares swivelling from me to the girl and back again. Only in Brighton!

Of course. That's it! I lurched to my feet.

The girl, dark blond strands of hair whipping about her shoulders, blipped off the screen of my vision around the corner. The girl . . . the young man. . . . heads bent at exactly the same angle, their pleasing faces stamped with exactly the same expression . . .

"Yes!" Half wearing my scarf and coat, my shoulder bag dragging on the floor, I tore out the door.

They had <u>got</u> to meet!

*   *   *

Still struggling with a coat that was trying to turn into a sail, I bucketed after the girl down one of the quaint narrow alleys known collectively as the Brighton Lanes. Tourists and shoppers swirled around me. It seemed a fruitless quest. And then, over the shoulder of a pimply adolescent wrestling with his West Ham United scarf, I caught a glimpse of Icelandic runes and a strand of blond hair, poised vertically like a cat's tail as it disappeared round the corner of the lane down to my left.

I collided with the adolescent. He hurled four-letter abuse at me as I barged past. My eagerness almost launched me into the air. I had the sail, you see, but not the rudder.

When I caught up with the girl, she was absently staring into an antique shop window.

Desperate situations call for desperate measures. I threw my handbag on to her foot.

"Ow!"

"Sorry," I shouted over the racket of the wind. I leaned forward solicitously. "All right, dear?"

"Am I supposed to say 'Never mind, I've got another foot?'" she shouted back, as she bent to peer at the outraged toes. She lost her balance, hopped, and was almost blown over by the wind. She turned to glare at me. "Can't you . . . ?"

She tailed off. Her gaze took in what I hoped was a distraught expression of sincerity.

"I really am sorry," I shouted. "I was trying to do my coat up. But in this wind"—I gestured to the empty air—"I couldn't manage . . . well, I . . . the bag just . . ."

Her distracted air of annoyance dissolved. I can always do that. Her expression became earnest with remorse. "It's all right, really." She grinned charmingly at me and turned her gaze back to the window.

A sense of desperation seized me. I'm nothing if not resourceful. At a forceful blast of wind I proceeded to lose my balance entirely. I cannoned into her, bounced, and appeared to hit my head a resounding crack on the shop window, though I actually did it with a good thwack of my bag behind me. A very versatile blunt instrument. I slid to the ground in a daze.

"Oh God." Now she felt guilty. The girl was all worry and confusion.

A man with a concerned expression and a craggy face that vaguely reminded me of Tommy Lee Jones-- or was it Clint Eastwood?--tacked against the wind and zigzagged over to help me up. I flailed at him rudely. He bent and, pronouncing his words with care, asked me if I was all right.

The girl, looking relieved, was about to go.

In a panic, I put my lips to his ear. "Naff off."

He backed away and raised his eyebrows, studying my face. I winked at him.

"I . . . er . . . see." He gave me a quaint little bow, saluted, and plonked off down the alley, raincoat flapping.

"Oh dear." The girl was anxious. "Where do you live? Can I phone someone for you?"

I stared at her blankly.

"Can't you remember?" She took out her mobile phone.

"Oh no, no. I'm all right. I just need a nice cup of cappuccino. Won't you come with me, just for a minute or two? Just until I know I'm steady?"

It was the second time I had seen relief on her face.

"My name's Liz," she said.

She took my arm and helped me up. I wobbled for good measure. "Mine's Grace. My mother liked Grace Kelly."

I weaved into the Italian restaurant I had just left, Liz holding my unsteady elbow. The two bob-haired ladies were still there. Their eyebrows rose to the Botticelli reproduction ceiling. Liz caught the eye of a good-looking waiter and turned to order. I gave the ladies a saucy wink. Their lips pursed again.

As we sipped our cappuccinos, I unearthed some useful information. Liz was assistant manager of a travel agency not far away. I knew the one. I'd often stared at the offers in the window. She'd done well at only twenty-three. She was also very disgruntled with her boyfriend, Jay.

Well, I thought, I couldn't have come at a better time!

It seems that Jay was driving her crazy. He would get obsessions. First it was kickboxing, then ventriloquism, karaoke, saving the West Pier, rescuing greyhounds and finding them homes (very praiseworthy, that, I thought), chiropody . . .

"Chiropody?" I could feel my eyebrows meeting my hairline.

"He, er, loves the female foot," she said, and went off into gales of laughter.

The two ladies demonstrated their outrage with a loud grinding of chairs as they got up to leave.

"And now," she went on, "it's two new fads. He's busy writing letters to Peru . . ."

"Peru?"

"Pen-Pals Peru. It's a campaign to write to Peruvians who can't get on-line . . ."

"Peru?" I tried not to gape. "How, er, interesting." I couldn't imagine what the second fad might be. "*Two* new fads, you said?"

"The other is doing card tricks."

"Card tricks?" I repeated stupidly. "Card tricks?" What other fads might overcome him without warning? Sending off jokes to the manufacturers of Chinese fortune cookies?

Liz reckoned he was bored because he worked in a bank. He was obviously a wally (except for the greyhounds). And now he wanted to be David Blaine with a penchant for chiropody. However had he attracted a girl like Liz? Perhaps she had lovely feet and an endless supply of playing cards!

We exchanged addresses—I said I wanted to send her a Christmas card--and we parted on friendly, if hurried terms. She had to get back to work. Yes, a very nice girl indeed. Definitely in need of a change in the romance department. That left me with the other half of the problem. How to get her together with the attractive young man I had seen earlier?

I had made sure we sat by the window so that I could spot him if he went by. Lord knows what I was going to do if he did.

Of course, he was nowhere in sight.

I thought perhaps if I wandered about a bit I might run into him. I didn't. But I did a lot more wandering about than I had anticipated.

Oh dear! I am probably creating the impression that I'm some sort of "bag" lady. Well in the sense that my bag is an essential part of my "look" and matches my shoes—yes. In the sense that I carry all my worldly goods in it, push an old pram and have no fixed abode—no. And I'm not *that* old. And I do own a car.

Yes, the car. Which brings me back to what I was saying earlier. I did a lot more wandering about than I had anticipated. Let me put it this way. Have you ever forgotten where you parked it?

I had found a space and bought a voucher. But where?

I finally had no option but to go to the police station. I did manage to find that. The young constable on the desk looked unsympathetic. I could see he was having a bad day.

"You've . . . misplaced your car, have you, madam?"

I decided on distraught sincerity.

He warmed. "Now that's a shame." (It always works, as I said.) "Are you a visitor to Brighton?"

"I'm afraid I live here. Well, in Hove."

"Ah."

I wasn't sure what he meant by that.

"I come into town from time to time because . . . because . . . Brighton has such colourful characters." I paused. He was staring at me fixedly. "I enjoy watching them."

His eye took in briefly the drunk hunched in the corner trying to sing "Dancing Queen", and the thirty-something male effing and blinding at a policewoman at the other end of the counter.

"I mean the crowds," I added hastily. I rushed on, "My vouchers will be running out about now, and I don't want to get a ticket. Oh dear."

"Right." Clearing his throat, he opened a large map of the town centre and spread it across the counter. We pored over it. He had to look at it upside-down. "So what's the most significant landmark you can remember?"

"Um, a mini-market next door to a florist." I sniffled.

"Hmm. Now don't upset yourself. I'm sure we can find it for you."

I heard a door open behind him. I sensed a pause.

"Find what?"

It was a new voice, but there was something vaguely familiar about it. I looked up. Straight into the eyes of Tommy Lee Jones--or was it Clint Eastwood?

"Afternoon, Inspector," said the constable (Inspector? Oh God!). "This lady has lost her car. I'm endeavouring to locate it for her."

"I see." The Inspector studied me thoughtfully, a gleam in his eye. "We must certainly try. It wouldn't do for us to tell her to 'naff off', now would it?"

"Sir?" The constable looked confused.

I looked for a hole in the floor. Where are holes in the floor when you need them? Probably with the lost cars.

I looked about. The aggressive male had just marched out. The policewoman, with a colleague's help, was firmly propelling the drunk, still singing, through double doors at the end. I don't know what I expected, but there was no escape in sight.

"I . . . er . . . Oh f . . . dear." I was flustered.

It got worse.

The Inspector was apparently asking me my name for the second time.

"Pond. Grace Pond."

The gleam in his eye disappeared. "That's amazing. I'm Q!" His eyes narrowed. "Do you have some identification?" He folded his arms. At that point he looked less like Q and more like the Man With No Name.

"No, really, I wasn't trying to be funny. Gerald Pond, of "Pond and Wyman", was my husband. And I'm Grace." I paused, then rushed on, "I'm very sorry about this afternoon, I mean . . ." I swallowed, ". . . I didn't mean to be rude but you see it was a matter of some urgency . . . awkward . . ." I tailed off miserably.

"You know this lady, sir?" the constable chimed in.

"Well, yes. No. Never mind, Peterson."

"Yes, sir." Peterson occupied himself with some paperwork.

"Look," I said to the suspicion of a glint in his eye, as I applied "distraught sincerity" for the third time that day, "I'd really like to explain."

I did my best.

When I got to the end of my story he was looking at me oddly. "So you see," I added, "you came along at exactly the wrong moment."

"And you just . . . *follow* people?"

"Did you know Greta Garbo used to do the same thing."

I thought he was suppressing a smile. He studied me. He was looking into my eyes in a very disconcerting way. Perhaps my mascara had run.

He offered me his hand. "Inspector Robert . . . Bob . . . Fielding."

I smiled back. His hand was warm and firm. Then my face fell. "My car."

Ten minutes later, with the help of a question and answer session, the map, and the intrepid inspector, we did manage to figure out where I had left it. I expressed my gratitude. He put out his hand again. "Well, er, if you ever lose your car again, you'll know where to come."

Did he seem a little reluctant, just when he was on the point of getting rid of me, or was it my imagination? I had the feeling he was about to say something further, when the cheery policewoman he had sent for joined us. He gave me that odd little bow and disappeared.

The policewoman drove me back to my car, making a sympathetic face as she left me at the curb. A summons fluttered under the windshield wipers. The car looked forlorn, its headlamps blank with reproach. I gave up. Time to de-stress.

I left the parking ticket on the car, took exact note of where I was, and clutching my map headed down to the Odeon on the sea front. By the time I left the cinema two hours later, I felt better. Mindless mayhem is so refreshing. But I felt the compulsive need for a cup of tea and a giant piece of coffee cake, as you do. I knew just the place. It was in the Lanes, not too far from the Italian restaurant.

The gale had abated. The tourists were out in force and the locals in a shopping frenzy. I was shoved, pushed, waltzed round, saluted, and yes--there he was again--persecuted by, I swear, the same mega-decibel screaming kid who seems to follow me on planes, into lifts, and especially into supermarkets.

Willowy girls in tattered jeans swept past me. A few marauding yaks shoved past. Occasional lone wolves with red-rimmed eyes and a spaced-out expression hugged the shop fronts, as if afraid they might fall down. Oh Brighton, Brighton. But I was thinking about the cake. That, and a stiff breeze behind me, improved my progress up North Street no end.

I'm sure there was another factor as well. I suddenly realised I was about to pass the travel agency where Liz worked. I stopped dead. A dangerous decision in a crowd.

"Hey, you crazy woman", said a dark brown voice as I collided with a dark brown man in Nigerian robes. He carried a Royal Pavilion shopping bag and a camera. He gave me a toothy grin.

I mumbled an apology, and pushing through clumps of people in a bus queue, reached the travel agency window. I pressed my face against the glass and shielded my eyes. It was not easy to see past the extravagant offers of a fortnight in Alicante and coach trips to Lapland. But there was Liz. I paused, riveted. She was standing behind her desk, in close discussion with a lanky young man she seemed to know well. Too well. A chilling thought struck me. This couldn't be the eccentric Jay, could it? The card trick fanatic with the pen pals in Peru?

I knocked on the window, but she did not take her eyes from his face. Two other agents, however, looked up enquiringly. I pointed at Liz, mouthed words, and banged harder.

"My dad says you shouldn't knock on people's windows and make faces."

My head swivelled in time to catch the eye of a boy of about eight.

"You're a yobbo!" he hissed.

"Alex, come *on*. We'll miss the bus."

He trailed off in pursuit of a harassed woman who was trying to run while manoeuvring a toddler and a pushchair. The boy made a rude gesture at me behind his back.

Bemused, I turned back to the window in time to see the mystery man plant a smacker on Liz's mouth. She did not object.

Of course, he could have been her brother, brother-in-law, cousin, best friend's brother, best friend's brother-in-law, brother's best friend . . . Even I could see I would drive myself mad.

I moved reluctantly on to the teashop, although the prospect of cake had suddenly gone stale. The wind had left my sails. I was in the doldrums.

With my elbows on the cream lace tablecloth, my chin cupped in my hands, the pot of tea getting cold and a cress sandwich uneaten, I tried to assess the situation. Irritatingly, my mind kept drifting to Inspector Fielding. The way he looked straight at me and twinkled was a bit disturbing. My God, what was I smiling at?

I sighed and waved the Inspector's image away like cigarette smoke. I must turn my attention to the business in hand. The question was: would I ever track down the promising young man I had decided would be just right for Liz? Would Liz be interested anyway, even if I did? Perhaps I could have a party?

Contrary to what you might suspect, I do actually know quite a lot of people. And some of them are respectable. I could invite him and Liz separately, then introduce them. I could even invite . . . A craggy face drifted into my mind. No. I fanned the image away yet again.

The waitress came over to ask if an insect was bothering me.

I found my car easily this time. I thought it looked even more forlorn than before, but of course that was probably me. I stuffed the summons in my bag and drove off. Too late I realised I would be caught in the rush hour traffic. Cars closed in behind me. The thirty miles an hour speed limit dropped to eight. I sighed and stared out at the darkening sea.

As I went to switch on my sidelights, I happened to glance at the petrol gauge and froze.

The warning light was on, the needle well past the E. I can't think how I missed it before. Oh God. That was all I needed. An empty tank!

The wind had dropped and it was starting to rain. Visions of a soggy trudge in the dark to the nearest petrol station, wherever that was, followed by the tramp back lugging a hefty can of petrol swam before my eyes. Knowing me, I could even get lost. I made my decision. Sainsbury's had a huge petrol station and best of all I knew where it was. I just needed a shortcut.

I swerved off the coast road and prayed to everybody, including Elvis and the Dalai Lama. It turned out to be amazingly effective. There stood Sainsbury's, flooded with light. It beckoned like Heaven. My legs felt rubbery with relief as I got out of the car. I filled the tank. Then I walked over and took my place in a queue for the counter.

There were two parallel queues. I gazed idly, assessing the other customers for the usual attitudes: annoyance, blank martyrdom, relief (like mine), foot and finger tapping, humming . . .

I stopped in mid hum. I felt myself strangle. My mouth opened and closed like a fish. There, joining the other queue, the same expression of preoccupation on his face as when he had passed the Italian restaurant window, stood the young man who had been so much on my mind.

My mind raced. What to do?

I reached my till first. The cashier was a bored twenty something, wearing sunglasses and chewing a toothpick. He looked like a reject from "The Matrix". The omens did not look encouraging. Well . . . nothing venture . . . Hastily, I pocketed the credit card I had been about to hand over. Instead, I fumbled in my bag, muttering.

Out of the corner of my eye I could see the young man I wanted to match up with Liz about to move up to his cashier. I looked up. Then, dramatically, I suddenly noticed him.

"Nick," I cried, "Nick. Thank goodness you're here. I've come out without my credit card or chequebook, and I've only got three pounds to my name."

The young man stared. He turned to look behind him, then back at me. I darted across and grabbed his arm.

"I'm so lucky to have run into you. How's your poor mother? Is she any better? Could you possibly help a fool of a woman in distress? I've just filled up my tank."

I could see him thinking I was probably several litres short of full.

"I'd be ever so grateful, dear." I was nearly out of breath with anxiety. I risked a quick look at *my* cashier, who had taken the toothpick out of his mouth and was looking peevish.

"I'm afraid . . ." Nick began. It was a pleasant, educated voice ". . . I'm afraid I'm *not* Nick, unfortunately." A firm voice, the sort of voice, perhaps, that is used to being in charge. I was secretly delighted.

"Not Nick? Of course you are. Goodness me, I only saw you two days ago at the vet's, remember? Has Crusher recovered?"

I was ruining the health of his entire family.

He seemed taken aback. "I think perhaps you've made a mistake." The word held a suggestion of steel as he removed my hand from his arm. Clearly I had to be a con artist.

My cashier chimed in. "Look, exactly how're you goin' to pay for your petrol?" I clutched my throat and looked upset.

"Nick" looked behind him at the lengthening queue and moved up hastily, preparing to settle his own bill. Panic gripped me. I pushed between him and the counter, effectively cutting him off. For the fourth time that day, I turned to distraught sincerity.

"I know this is embarrassing for you, Nick dear. I don't know where to put myself. But you know I'll pay it back tomorrow morning." My voice quavered as I pulled out my handkerchief. "I can bring it round and give it to your poor mother, if that would be more convenient. How is she, did you say? I do so hate getting into debt." I fought back the tears. "Oh this is awful."

"Get a move on," came a gravelly voice from the back. "Some of us don't want to be here til midnight." There was a chorus of low muttering.

He hesitated.

"Excuse me." It was Nick's cashier, a youngish woman who kept hooking her hair behind her ear. "Look, sir, could you either pay for your petrol or get out of the queue please?"

My cashier took off his sunglasses and droned with finality: "Sorry, but I'm goin' to have to call security, madam."

"Oh for God's sake," came a shout from the back, "lend her the money, tosser!"

Nicholas gritted his teeth. Without a word, he pushed round me, offered the girl his credit card and punched in his pin number. My heart sank. Instantly I pictured myself frogmarched by security men to a grey interrogation room. But instead of marching out the door, the next thing Nick did was to stomp across to my queue and punch in the same pin number for me.

I felt an iron grip on my arm as he propelled me outside to a smattering of applause.

"Right, now perhaps you'll tell me what the hell is going on? How about a name?"

"I'm Grace. Grace P. . . I'm a widow. Mrs. Pond. Please, could I just sit down? You tell me your address and I'll pay you tomorrow. Here, take my watch as collateral."

"I thought you knew my address," he said in a dangerously quiet voice. "And let me clarify something else. I do not have a dog called Crusher, and my mother, who enjoys excellent health, lives in France."

Better to break the deadlock. People from the queue would be coming out any minute. "Just a quick cup of tea, dear." I started towards the cafeteria across the car park. "I must sit down."

Assuming he hoped to see his fifty pounds again, and since he could hardly assault me in public, he had no choice but to follow. He ordered two teas. Then he demanded my keys and went back to park both cars away from the pumps. He returned and sat down. We faced each other in silence over the teacups.

I decided I would have to come clean.

"I'm sorry, really I am," I said in my normal voice. "I *know* you don't know me, and I don't know you. I have the money in my bag." I rummaged and handed him a fistful of notes. He was about to say something (probably about extortion), but I cut him off.

"I'm a psychologist," I blurted. "I'm studying how people behave in queues, so I do things sometimes just to see what will happen."

He leaned back in his chair and steepled his fingers, weighing me up like a bank manager.

"May I include you in my study?" I treated him to my most sincere smile.

He scrutinised my face.

"Look," I went on, "this is my address, here on my driving license. I'm not a crook. Really."

He leaned forward. I half expected him to say I had been turned down for a loan. Instead, very slowly, he did the oddest thing imaginable. He grinned. Oh yes, Liz would like him. I was sure of it.

Now all I had to do was get them together. I could probably . . .

"I'm James Tilton." He offered me his hand. "Here's my card."

My God! He really was a bank manager! I was just deciding that having a party would be a very good idea when, for the third time that day, I heard a familiar voice behind me.

Hastily I dropped a serviette and, diving to retrieve it, craned my neck from under the table. Bearing down on us, his arm full of groceries and a hand outstretched, was a smiling Inspector Fielding.

"Evening, James. How's my overdraft?"

James rose and shook hands. "Bob! How was the dinner?" They shook hands. "Did they miss me?"

"Indeed they did. I . . ." The inspector's voice tailed off as my face emerged from under the table. I gave him a wobbly smile.

"Grace!"

"You two know each other?"

"It's a long story," he replied.

"Yes," said James wryly, "I'll bet it is. Can't wait to hear it. Please, join us." He took out his wallet, waving Bob Fielding to a chair. As he did so, some papers fluttered to the floor. Bob pointed.

"No," said James, misunderstanding. "My treat. I insist. That chocolate cake's been waiting for us all day." He strode off to the counter.

Bob picked up an envelope. "This fell out of his pocket. It's a very exotic stamp."

I suddenly felt peculiar.

"What's the matter?"

"Matter? I . . . oh, I . . . nothing. I just thought . . ." I paused, as my eye caught something else under James's chair. Suddenly I felt as if I'd been going down in a lift too fast. As the inspector half got up to look, a shudder of merriment rippled up my throat and burst into hysterical laughter.

He sat down again, all concern. "Grace, are you all right?"

My shoulders shook. "I . . . I . . . think," I spluttered finally, "I need something a bit stronger than tea." If this sounded like a brazen come-on, I didn't blush about it until later.

"I'd be delighted," he twinkled at once. "There's a nice pub up the road. And it's my night off," he added. "A bit uninspiring, going home to the cat."

We smiled at one another.

"Just a quick cuppa with James first, eh?" he added. "To be polite. Nice chap."

"Yes, he is," I giggled. "A bit odd, though." I started laughing again.

He raised his eyebrows enquiringly. "Odd?"

I tapped the envelope on the table. "It's from Peru."

"So it is." He looked puzzled.

Then I bent down and retrieved the second item from the floor.

It was the Jack of Hearts.

CROSSING LINES

a.m.

Michael Bateson was a success. At a certain level, that is. Corporately speaking. He inhabited the world of affairs. He was self-contained, aloof. He never gave his money, his time, or himself. Except to the goddess who ordained his days.

So Michael Bateson lolled inviolate inside the crystal bubble of himself on the 7:25 to Victoria. He no more noticed the surges of activity around him than a rock registers the buffeting of the wind. Not the brisk jostling for a seat, the briefcases thumping on to racks, throat clearing, handkerchief hunting, bluff monosyllables, the snap of newspapers unfolding, smart phones clicking—none of the rituals of a scrupulously maintained anonymity. It was a ritual that he, too, maintained.

The train picked up speed. A brick factory whipped by. The bell clanged a harsh and diminishing vibrato.

A woman with bobbed hair marched down the carriage cradling a pink folder. Her shoulder bag thudded against his temple. It was a personal intrusion that prompted him to look up and glare at her retreating back. She flung open the dividing door and caught his eye as she turned to gaze at the long rectangle of faces. Her chin was raised, her mouth faintly set in an expression that might have been disappointment. Or perhaps contempt.

Abruptly, she turned on her heel, hair swinging, and vanished. The door clunked shut behind her. A hint of gillyflowers hovered in the air. It asserted itself for the briefest of moments before subsiding into the miasma of coffee.

Michael Bateson, of upper middle management, stared at the spot where she had disappeared. "Eight years!" With complacent abstraction he examined his fingernails, his mind rattling into cherished grooves with the familiar juddering of the compartment. "Eight years!" He tapped his glasses up the bridge of his nose in gesture of self-congratulation. Yes. He'd done well. In spite of all those redundancies, The Corporation had wanted him, kept him on board. It was his due, after all. He was indispensable.

All part of the strategy.

But it was a tenuous romance. He wooed The Corporation like a lover. He served Her with established rituals, like some primeval priest. He was abject before Her power to humiliate and reject him.

However, Michael Bateson possessed one unlikely and engaging asset - as unexpected in the desert of his under-control self as a camel in the Arctic. He had the most infectious of laughs. Though he generated it with care, like his charm - convincing, insubstantial - and though it began obediently on cue, he sometimes found it acquiring a disturbing reality, welling up of its own accord, grasping at a genuine amusement that seemed to geyser up from somewhere deep in memory. Unnerved, he always retreated to the safety of the crystal bubble, his invisible igloo. He kept the untidy, disorganised world at bay. But the world found him pleasant enough.

"Tickets please." A corpulent black conductor leaned across and scanned his pass with perfunctory care. "Tickets."

The train was on time this morning. He would be there even earlier than usual. And he'd polished off that two-day backup last night. Inevitably, his gaze flicked to the sleek briefcase on the rack opposite. The Christmas present of two years ago from Fran. It held his attention just a fraction too long. At once, like a genie, her troubled features rose to reproach him. He shifted with irritation in the too-small space next to the window. Somebody's arm dug into his ribs. With a determined effort he attempted to wrestle her image back into oblivion. It was like trying to cram a protesting cat into a sack.

He ran a hand through greying hair and gazed at the faint outline of himself in the window, a ghostly self, invaded from time to time by rearing elms and hedgerows tumescent with hawthorn.

On the other side of the carriage, an extraordinary May morning drenched waking fields in a haze of gold. Old tin sheds, defiant in burgeoning allotments, winked under the gilded light like polish. It poured over dustbin lids and empty swings, car parks, and apartment blocks with the sweetness of melting toffee. It trickled like coins among the leaves. Dozing sheep wore a silver nimbus. And everywhere, the commonplace became unique.

Michael Bateson saw only a runnel of soot on the window. He lolled unmoving. Calm. His thumbs alone, rotating around each other with obsessive speed, betrayed the compulsive momentum of his thoughts. His eye registered the brief image of a woman in a grey blouse hanging out washing. She seemed to stand immobile, impervious to the railway clatter, her clothes peg the momentary focus of her world. Two small boys grappled in a junk-filled garden. A brown dog waited at a door, beside two empty milk bottles that glinted like stars.

He had planned his life. With a rational approach you could achieve anything. If people planned their lives they wouldn't get unwelcome surprises. The dim shadow of a precipice hurtled towards him. Hastily his mind veered, then rushed full tilt and crossed the gulf, galloping on. These people with insurmountable problems! These people who almost died of loneliness, or who thought they were dying of love. Or lack of it! These people who never had any money! Cod's bloody wallop!

Michal Bateson had no sympathy with frailty. Even illness offended him. It was, after all, a weakness. Failure had a simple cause:--a lamentable lack of planning. Ignorance, poverty, drunkenness, bewilderment, compulsive gambling, mental distress— he stuffed them all into the same neat file: OWN BLOODY FAULT. Silly buggers.

The cat stirred and tried to get out of the sack. He clenched his teeth. Swimming to his feet against the momentum of the train, he grasped the window over the nearest door and wrenched it shut. Two of his fellow travellers looked up sharply from their phones. He lurched back to his seat, avoiding contact with the sleeve of his faceless travel companion with the ease of long practice. He clenched his fists, braced himself. The sack went flying. The cat leaped.

He closed his eyes.

She came at me like a madwoman. Like a madwoman. The astonishment always returned with each re-enactment, like some bizarre musical score. What was it she wanted, Fran? What? They're always after something, women. What did I do? Came at me with that look on her face, trying to beat me round the head with the heel of her shoe. Two and a half inch heels! I was a good provider. I've done my bit. Didn't run after other women.

He remembered the stab of her heel against his collarbone.

"Fran, stop it! Fran! You're irrational."

Clearly he recalled his intent—to knock the bloody shoe out of her hand and keep it away from his face. He saw her flail at him. Saw himself swing the back of his hand in a deflecting arc. Felt again the shock as it connected unexpectedly with her face. He watched her spin and fall, like an ice skater. She sat crumpled, dumbfounded, staring at him. Blood edged down the corner of her mouth. It gushed from her nose. In the dead silence he was aware that he was holding his breath. The silence deepened.

A fly crawled up the picture of the two of them skiing in Colorado on a business trip. The drone of a jet, just audible, pinpointed the stillness of the room as its silhouette in the sky pinpointed infinity. He was aware of his own breath, suddenly released, a thudding in his temples, pain at the back of his eyes. He noted with vague annoyance that the wine stain at the edge of the carpet looked darker. Somewhere, beyond The Avenue, an ice cream van tinkled an incongruous ditty.

Groping for leverage she scrambled to her feet. He remembered thinking how the movement—clumsy, abrupt—seemed out of character. A book about Icelandic horses pitched to the floor as the nest table on which it lay overturned. The red welt from his hand blared like some tribal tattoo across her cheek.

Blood spattered the bodice of her top and dripped on to her sleeve.

"You bastard!" The low note, almost a whisper, trembled with unresolved malice. "You get away with it all the time, don't you Micky? Don't you?" Her voice shot up the scale. "Bastard!" The note shrilled to a scream. "You're killing me!"

She ran at him. "You stupid . . ." She clawed at his face. He lifted his arm in a protective gesture. A backhanded gesture. She retreated at once, her face caught between bewilderment and frenzy.

"It's not what I . . . Fran . . . I didn't . . . Frannie . . ."

She drowned his words. "Well this is one thing you're not going to get away with, Micky!"

He registered the sharp camera click impression of her chalk-white face. For a frozen second he saw himself reflected in her darkened pupils. She gazed back at him with an outrage too deadly for speech. Then she turned, stumbling in her one shoe, and plunged towards the door. Her hair swung out as she tore it open. She hurled herself through and was gone.

He stood riveted. Heard the jingle of keys. Heard the front door bang, her car start, pull away, fade in the distance.

He picked up the shoe, turned it over in his hands, saw himself standing there looking foolish, a pantomime parody. The cream shoe, no glass slipper, dropped from his hand.

That had been one of the worst nights of his life. He had spent it in a police cell. She had shopped him all right and tight. It had done him no good at all when he'd tried to tell them he hadn't intended assault.

"I see." A bored, jarringly youthful face studied him with contempt. "Would you like to explain that, sir?"

He'd got off because it hadn't been hard to prove she was unstable. Unstable? Incomprehensible, for Christ's sake. She'd had treatment, after all.

When she'd cleared off to New Zealand with a ne'er-do-well nine years her junior he'd been well shut of her. Going for him not with a plate hurled across the room, but a high-heeled shoe! Hand to hand combat, that was what she'd wanted. Contact. Funny, that.

With a determined shove he jammed the cat back in the sack. He opened his eyes.

"Oh fuck it!" She was crazy. His mind subsided, merging with the hypnotic rhythms of the train.

*   *   *

p.m.

Adelaide Last flopped into the seat next to the window, crossed her legs and wedged the pink folder against her knee. She longed to get rid of her shoes and put her feet up. For the last hour, like The Little Mermaid, she had been teetering on knives. She would like to have thrown the damn shoes out the window.

She surveyed her travel companions with some relief. She would be late getting home but she had successfully avoided the lemming hour. Just a shade too late now for most of the charging automatons, faces as dispiriting as Vaseline, who had crammed the train that morning.

A band of pressure, like a too-tight hat, squeezed harder around her forehead, releasing mean little jabs of pain. Closing her eyes, she leaned forward and began to massage the back of her neck with both hands. The bobbed hair jounced. She thought again of the tight grey brigade that morning, with their tight grey expressions, blue shirts, shoes scuffed in a thousand escalator scrums. And the female counterparts in the careful outfits, in careful, unobtrusive shades, with the carefully applied lipstick and pulled-back hair. A passive army, finding out what the world was doing in "The Telegraph" or "The Independent", or, more furtively, "The Mail". A uniformed consignment of lifers.

Mentally she shuddered. She wasn't wholly at liberty herself, yet. Only, as it were, paroled. It was hard.

That morning she had deliberately thumped somebody she had passed in the compartment with her shoulder bag. She had anticipated the usual bovine resilience to contact. This one had glared. Not much of a response, but better than nothing. She had looked at the other occupants of the compartment. Staring at the dreary ranks she had pitied them in their narrowness. "Like looking at myself," she thought. She hated them for every stricture that had been placed upon herself and every obliteration she had suffered in the name of concurrence. Somebody else's definitions. Somebody else's fixations. Somebody else's expectations. Somebody else's lack of awareness.

Drew Berringer's.

He was a prominent American attorney, a workaholic whose addiction was every bit as deadly as amphetamines or AIDS. And she had married him. He took work on holiday. He worked at home in his study every night of the week. If she wanted to talk to him it had to go down in his diary. He worked on Saturdays. He worked on Sunday afternoons. And yet it was stability she had hoped for as his wife. He had been clever, steady, devoted, and when she met him she had been so drained, so lost.

He had pursued her with a single-mindedness that bordered on the compulsive. Once he caught her, however, he merely heaved a sigh of relief and put her in a display cupboard with a sign, "not needed until required". That meant dinner parties, charity benefits and other suitable occasions. The rest of the time she felt like a robot with the key removed.

She tried to work. But she had chopped and changed too much already. Her professional skills atrophied and she felt herself becoming obsolete. Adelaide's pleasure, however, which had developed late, had been as unlikely as it was fulfilling— singing. She began to look for work in cabaret, as she had done once before, when . . . when . . .

"Adelaide, for Chrissake! You're an educated woman. What are you trying to do to me? The wives of prominent attorneys do not, I repeat, NOT, sing in cabarets. How do you think it would look? Even if you manage to get someone to hire you, which I doubt."

Not cowardly, but simply too tired to marshal the energy to oppose him, she acquiesced. She had already lost the very fabric of her being.

Which is not to say that she didn't make scenes.

"You want too much, Adelaide!"

"And you want too little. All from Armani!" Her voice rose to a scream. "You're killing me!"

He dodged as a milk jug flew over his head and gouged a chunk of plaster from the wall. She tried to heave the vacuum cleaner at him as well, but its weight defeated her.

"Shit! Goddamn crazy broad!"

She hurled a law book at him.

It was the only way she could get his attention.

He lived in a crystal bubble, an invisible igloo-- seeing but not perceiving, hearing but not listening, busy but not involved. She stuck it for nine years. She stuck it because she was burnt out, because she somehow felt it must be her fault; and because, of all the sweetest ideals that we lay upon the altar of the heart, what Adelaide had lost was hope.

Looking back now, she wondered if she had been quite sane. When, at last, she left him, he wrote her impassioned letters. She had to request an unlisted phone number to get any sleep. He threatened a new male friend of hers with assault. "Bitch, bitch, bitch . . . !" He followed her to a restaurant and made a scene. He begged and pleaded with her to come back to him. He sent roses. He obstructed divorce.

She fought for a year to get it. She came away from the marriage after ten years with nothing but a few flickering sparks. At thirty-eight, Adelaide came face to face with the devastating awareness of wasted potential. She could no longer remember what it felt like to function normally, realistically, at optimum capacity, expecting success, meeting life head on.

Three months after the final decree, Andrew Berringer remarried. Someone he had only met six weeks ago. No doubt he imagined himself in love again. She thought of that Rupert Brook poem she had learned at school:

> "And I shall find some girl perhaps,
> And a better one than you . . .
> Something, something, something . . .
> And I dare say she will do."

It was apt.

Six months ago, she had come back to England.

The train shuddered, grinding out of Victoria. It picked up speed, hesitated, slowed, accelerated again. The pink folder shot to the floor, catching the middle-aged man opposite her on the shin. Sleeves rolled up. Sinewy arms like ropes. Baggy jeans, a seamed face.

"Oh, I'm so sorr . . ."

"Hey, don't fret yerself now." The Aussie voice matched the walnut tan. He picked up the folder and handed it to her with a little nod. "Life's a bitch, ain' it." He smiled without reservation. Her mouth twitched doubtfully. Most people's reactions weren't so instantly favourable. Not at first.

It's my damn face.

Her face was certainly unfortunate. Not that the features were ugly, or irregular. On the contrary. But there was a natural arrogance to her expression that put people off. Worse, in repose the corners of her mouth turned slightly down. This, combined with a small frown line between her brows, lent an inveterate petulance to her features, which most of the time she was not experiencing in the least. When in real distress, her face assumed a look of tragedy so intense that it looked like bad acting.

Adelaide had suffered severely for her face. It had infuriated teachers, who accused her of surliness when she had merely been listening with attention. It antagonised strangers, and threw down the gauntlet to waitresses. She had been accused of imperiousness. When she tried to counter the effect, she was written off as patronising.

But Adelaides's face did not always discourage further investigation. Not when she smiled. The change then was startling. So startling that it had caused a number of people to pause in mid-sentence, for animation lent her face a strikingly odd beauty. Her mouth twitched now at the Australian and curved into her engagingly sudden grin. "Life's a bitch, you're right about that."

His eyes widened. He beamed back, scratched his arm again, checked his watch and settled down comfortably with a Lee Child paperback.

Clapham and Battersea shambled past in Dickensian confinement. Each little rectangular garden, with its lawn or old motorbike parts, ginger cat or washing line, like a soul flashing an SOS. A gem-like obstinacy in the scrimmage of brick and chimney pots.

With the thinning of the houses came a subtle change in the light. "A watercolour," thought Adelaide. "England is like a watercolour." It was the only pang of belonging she had had since coming home. "I seem to have spent half my life on journeys of one sort or another. Never arriving."

An empty playground spun by. A few clouds were gathering in the west.

"Like being on a train for ever, caught in some wobbling corridor between glass panes that let you see so much and participate so little before you're swallowed up in the final goddamned tunnel!" The familiar shroud of despair settled on her like an old coat.

Evening fields churned past. She found the motion dizzying to a mind already tired out by a dispiriting day. Interviews! An exercise in humiliation. She sighed, re-crossed her legs, fidgeted. A girl pedalled up a farm track. In the next field a woman strode out in wellingtons, with a walking stick and a red setter. Two bay horses proceeded to race each other round a field and through a gap into the next. Just for the hell of it! Adelaide craned her neck in amazement. She could still see them, tails streaming, heads up, hind legs skittering.

"Why do you want this job?"

"I bloody don't!"

No, she hadn't said that. Only the usual stuff about commitment . . . matches my qualifications . . . will use my skills . . . stimulating . . . And she did want the job. Well, she needed it. Money was tight. She'd be good at it. That she knew, even if they didn't. Beyond that, she didn't care much.

She had heard the litany of queries in the minds of the interview board members as clearly as if they had voiced them. It was like sitting in the dock before a row of prosecuting QC's.

She had been able to supply no one for the defence but herself.

"Why did you change jobs?"

"Might as well do one job as another. I was lost. I felt too much and did too little. A common enough disease, counsellor."

"And do you have any money to show for all this . . . floundering about?"

"You know I don't."

"You really haven't made much of your life in any sense, have you? No goals. No sense of ambition. In short, members of the jury, no bloody sense."

"You're probably right. I've achieved nothing at all."

Then another would have a go.

"Not part of the race, eh?"

"The human race?"

"The Life race."

"Oh, I'm in it, still picking myself up from the starting block when everyone else is out of sight."

Miss Last . . . Or do you prefer Ms? *I, er, see you're not even a couple."*

"I was. Twice."

"Ah, so you can't sustain relationships either?"

"I've just got a dog now."

"I see. Reluctant to take emotional risks, is that right? Members of the jury, what we have here is an immature personality, too selfish to give to others . . . Miss Last, why are you laughing?"

No emotional risks!

Adelaide blinked rapidly. She groped for a handkerchief.

Diagonally across from her, a woman paused in her reading. Pleasant blue eyes crinkled. Adelaide guessed that she must be in her fifties. But her face revealed a shocking vapidity, like an unprinted page. There were a few lines. But they were not lines of character. Only of sleeping too much on the right side, or squinting in dim light. Where were the paragraphs, the exclamation marks, the capital letters, the question marks? It was a face that had never been lived in. Adelaide noted reddened hands and a wedding ring. But this was a woman who had never held a man in her arms, never felt despair . . .

A distant pain shot through her like an arrow, and was gone. She struggled to hold shut a door in her mind. It was old, scuffed, painted brown, and it smelled of the upper west side of Manhattan. She pushed hard against it, panting. It closed.

With relief she stared at the woman again, puzzling, sifting the possibilities. Suddenly she had it. Of course. That was it. She was looking at a nun in civvies.

Instantly, her triumph vanished like a switched-off light as another pain flared into her awareness like a locomotive. The old scuffed door flew open.

Laughter bubbled up into her consciousness.

"Get thee to a nunnery!"

She could hear him saying it, outraging that poor woman from Brooklyn when they had visited Greece together. They were in the amphitheatre at Epidaurus.

"Richie . . . "

The woman's husband charged to the attack. "Don't you talk dirty to my wife!" He looked around at a few interested tourists. "This guy's nuts."

"Sit on it, buddy!" said Justin in his best New York accent.

"Huh? What's your problem, pal?"

Justin sighed. "The language of Milton."

"Huh?"

"I think your husband has a touch of the sun . . . er . . . perhaps," volunteered a British professor to Adelaide. "I mean, I just thought . . . that is . . ."

"What makes you think I'm her husband?" retorted Justin, British to the core again. "This is my mistress. My wife has taken the kids to Bournemouth!"

"Oh dear! I'm most frightfully sorry."

"I'm not."

"Oh no, I mean . . ."

"He's just having a bit of a joke," said Adelaide desperately. "He's rehearsing a role. My husband is an actor."

"Oh, oh I see . . ."

Adelaide decided to quit while they were ahead. "Let's go back to the hotel, Justin."

He winked at an Italian tourist. "She's going to have her way with me."

The man nodded approvingly. "I shoulda be so lucky." He pinched her bottom.

"Justin, he just pinched my . . ."

"Get me a sword!"

The American woman grabbed Adelaide's arm, convinced she was about to witness a major incident. "I don't think you should go with him, honey."

"It's all right", said Adelaide. "Just a little too much Ouzo."

"Metaxa, every time!" roared Justin, in his most fulminating stage voice.

"That's disgusting!" The American woman reddened.

"You're right. It's my thespian panache!"

"Oh my god, he's a pervert. Richie . . ."

"We're not listening to any more of this filth," said Richie."

"Filth?" retorted Justin. "Have you seen Hoboken?"

Somehow she managed to drag him away. By the time they reached the car, they were fighting hysterics.

Justin. The great irony had never ceased to fill her with wonder. That the most genuinely real individual she had ever known was an actor, a man whose profession had been the manufacture of pretence. Justin. He had been her first husband.

Her parents' only comment, by letter, had made disparaging reference to the sanity of a male choosing to earn his living "poncing about in make-up."

She'd met him in Peru on a university trip and gone back with him to New York. He'd been living there for five years. He had an American ex-wife. "She wanted my soul, pet. That's OK. But she wouldn't give me hers."

He had remarkable hands—long-fingered, firm. He had read everything, lived everything, felt everything. He wanted her to share it. He was a generous friend and a generous lover. He had an agreeably handsome face, and the rangy frame of a swimmer. He had a wicked wit, an incisive intellect, and a heart he was brave enough to show. He was a drunk. He nearly killed her with grief. And she had loved him with all her heart.

She could see now that it had already been too late when she met him. The flaw was there. Though, of course, she hadn't known it then. She had tried in every way to help him. But she couldn't do anything at all. Nothing. Only be there. Why?

Always the question. Never an answer. Why?

"You and your piss-elegant furniture. You make me want to throw up. Where's your fucking halo?" He hurled a bottle at the wall, took a step, fell over.

She knelt down. He reached up and tried to stroke her bare arm with torpid fingers.

"I'm sorry, Sunny. I'm sorr . . ." He started to cry. "I'm sorry."

"I know."

"Don't leave me. 'Sunny, one so true . . .'" And he had passed out on the floor.

Rescuing him, often unconscious, sometimes not, from bar room floors, car parks, gutters, and less savoury places, had endowed Adelaide with a dauntingly sharp tongue—colloquial, street-wise. Raunchy, even. It didn't go at all with her appearance of graceful fragility.

Frantic, loving, baffled, she watched him slowly disintegrate.

He wouldn't seek help. She arranged to have him taken to clinics. But each time he insisted on returning to the apartment. She had been told to lock him out. But she was too terrified he would disappear among the derelicts of the Bowery.

Then, as though he knew he had only one chance, he made a last effort himself. "Let's go home, Sunny. I miss it. You know, England, where all the people talk funny. Village greens and cricket matches. Awful, dear old Brum. Wouldn't you give anything to hear a Brummy accent? Maybe I could . . . Christ, I even miss "The Archers".

Transatlantic phone calls. Surreptitious conversations about clinics and convalescence and money. Living arrangements, contacts.

Her mother told her it was her own fault. "And you needn't bring him here, not even for a visit."

Adelaide had been singing old jazz standards at a little piano bar on East 79th Street.

She had achieved a small but devoted following. She made enough to give up one of her two "sensible" jobs downtown.

Justin came in whenever he could. Even at home, after some of his worst benders, he would take her hand and smile, "Come on, Sunny. Sing!" It seemed to bring him an odd kind of hope as well as pleasure, and it made her feel the same.

She would sing everything she could think of, including "Three Blind Mice" and "God Save The Queen". When she was fired for repeatedly failing to show up at the piano bar, he was distraught. He knew the reason.

But they were still able to scrape together a bit of cash, ready for their move across the Atlantic. Amazingly, Justin was still offered work. Not much. The odd film. He could no longer sustain stage performances eight times a week. And the more he slipped, the more he drank.

"Sunny, guess what! I've landed this job in Argentina. Only a four-day shoot. We don't leave for England until the thirtieth, so it will fit in just right. And we could use the money."

It was then that she had felt the first lizard stirrings of terror. He looked at her steadily, and what she had seen in his eyes had made her want to take all that she was, all that she had ever been, like a little paperweight of multi-coloured glass, and put it in his hand.

"Please don't go."

"I think I must, pet. It'll be fine." He looked at her again with the same expression.

"Better for you, you know . . ." He paused. "Get me out of your hair." He went on lightly, "I mean, you want to supervise the packing and so forth." He smiled. The knot in her throat relaxed. "Come on, Sunny. Sing!"

But at night, his body close and warm beside her in the dark, the terror came back.

Somewhere, deep in the mossy recesses of her innermost heart, she had known. She drove him to the airport. He looked better than he had for a long time. He sauntered over to a kiosk. "Look at this. A good old Bounty Bar. Haven't seen one of these for ages. For you." He bowed.

"I'll share it with you," she said. "Look, it's in two pieces anyway. One each. It'll be like a toast."

"No." He moved closer, looking down at her. "You eat yours and keep mine for me til I get back." He grinned and covered her hand with his. "It'll remind you there's always something to look forward to. Always! And don't you forget it." He kissed her forehead lightly, and was gone.

He phoned once, after his arrival. He sounded cheerful.

She was washing up when she got the second telephone call. She knew before anyone spoke that he was dead. She listened to the metallic voice on another continent. Her brain felt like a beach with the tide suddenly sucked out beyond the horizon. Before the tsunami.

"Middle of the Argentine pampas . . . flat land for miles . . . bizarre car accident . . . a head on collision . . . farm machinery . . ." He had been alone.

She had not stared at the floor in shock. She had not called a friend, desperate for comfort. She had not sat down with her head in her hands. She had not wept. She had thrown back her head and howled like a primeval animal. She howled like a demonic creature. She howled until her vocal chords were in tatters. She howled until neighbours broke down the door.

But she had come back to England with him after all. She had brought his body home.

He slept not far from the Avon, and in summer within the sound of leather on willow.

He was thirty-six.

Adelaide blinked hard several times. After his death she couldn't stay in England when they had made such plans for a fresh start together there. And she certainly couldn't stay in New York. She'd never again be able to sit in Barrymore's on West 46th Street, banging the table, listening to anecdotes of the stage on the Great White Way, having political arguments, laughing with their friends, watching the Broadway crowds. His absence was like a plain of ash stretching to every horizon.

So she moved to a small town across the river in New Jersey. She met a big city attorney named Andrew Berringer. Some time later, she married him.

Adelaide came fully awake with an unnerving jolt.

A face, the hair spiked like a green chrysanthemum, hovered inches from her own. A skull pendant swung within an inch of her mouth.

"Who's laid Adelaide? Who laid Adelaide . . . last?" he guffawed. Another youth with a beer can was holding her pink folder aloft. It had her name on the cover. There was no sign of the Aussie or the nun. She glanced at her watch. No, she hadn't missed her stop. Nowhere near, yet. She stared calmly into the boy's face with her most imperious expression. One eyebrow rose delicately.

"Hey!" The boy with the folder whinnied admiringly. You've got balls, love."

"And you won't have, in a minute. Give me that!" She held out her hand.

There was a splatter of male laughter. "Wheyheyhey! Go on, Eddie!"

How many of them were there? Four? Five? The boy with the spiked hair was wearing black jogger bottoms and an orange T-shirt with "Doom" in lurid pink across it. He was also wearing roller blades. He demonstrated a spin.

The boy holding her folder pushed the others aside and jammed a beer can into her extended hand.

"Yeah, Colin. Cool!"

Through the crush she caught sight of a man across the aisle. He cringed in his seat, flattening himself into the upholstery.

"Who's laid Adelaide?" The others took up the chant.

Doom Eddie shoved Colin out of the way. "Don't want your little drinky then, eh?"

She turned her gaze full upon him. Calmly, she stood the opened can on the window ledge and then tapped it over with her finger. Beer splashed onto the floor.

He laughed. "I just gotta lay Adelaide. Wanna fuck, love?" He rumba-ed over to the window, dominating the group. She could smell his breath.

She scanned his anatomy with crude precision, then reached up and grabbed. She smiled at him pityingly. "If only the rest of you were as big as your mouth!"

Eddie's face blanked. A second later a gang cheer went up. "Yaaaay. Woooo-ha!"

Eddie licked his lips, swigged his beer, rolled it round his mouth and spat it out over Adelaide's shoes. "Fucking bitch. What are you, darlin'? Fifty?" He jostled Colin and grabbed another beer from a boy behind him who was scratching his groin.

Adelaide seized her chance, rose, snatched the folder and flounced out of the compartment. She noted with satisfaction that the man in the seat across the aisle had flushed scarlet.

She knew they wouldn't follow. Eddie wouldn't risk losing face in front of his mates again. At least not while there were other people on the train. She sank into a seat two compartments further up, her head pounding. The seat opposite was empty. She kicked off her shoes, grateful finally to put her feet up. A stewardess and pilot sat across the aisle, bound for Gatwick, no doubt.

She still felt jangled, invaded. The experience had vividly recalled what it was like walking past the porn shops on 42nd Street. She took out a little bottle of perfume and dabbed her wrists and temples. The scent of gillyflowers filled the compartment.

Dispiritedly she opened the folder. It bulged with job paraphernalia. She felt as if she were climbing a mound of ice cream in combat boots. Total exhaustion began to creep through her body like a fatal injection. Interviews and yobs. Menopause and death next! "That's it, Adelaide, old duck. Oh stop it!" She clenched her jaw. "You're being irrational," as Drew would say.

What would Justin say?

Two empty soft drink cans rolled back and forth on the seat across the aisle, opposite the stewardess and pilot. They clinked together, like a bizarre toast.

Airports. That day of endings. "Always something to hope for. Always!" His voice came back to her across the reaches of time.

In his matchless way, he had made the most life-affirming of choices. His death had offered her freedom. "Your share . . ."

But her life had gone down other roads since then. All of them dead ends. And he had been dead such a long time.

"Oh, Justin. What would you say to your Sunny now?"

A mangled straw skittered under her seat. She looked down. A grubby newspaper lay in the aisle. On her left, on the ledge by the window, more litter. Something about the wrapper attracted her attention.

Absently, she reached for it.

*   *   *

a.m.

When Michael Bateson got off the train that morning, he had not expected his life to be changed. The collision, when it happened, brought him face to face with a greater stranger than Death. Himself.

It was because Nora Clegg was dawdling. In her best hat and new support stockings she was mumbling to herself as she rummaged through an enormous handbag smothered in ginger hairs. Nothing so ordinary as a cat or dog. Nora Clegg kept a family of guinea pigs on the living room sofa. She was a great favourite with her grandson, Micky, who counted the hours to his visits in the little flat in Golders Green.

Every few weeks, she would announce to the guinea pigs, and to nobody in particular, as if it had come to her like a bolt from the blue: "I'm off ta town ta see the queen, bless 'er." She would stand at the railings of Buckingham Palace, scrutinising the windows, nudging tourists, regaling them with a tabloid history of the royal family, and pointing out the Guards. "Lovely fellas!" Then she would walk down the Mall and feed the ducks in St James' Park. "And I love them white pelicans."

At 11:26, Michael Bateson, who had just made a token visit on behalf of The Corporation to a multinational office near Buckingham Palace Road, and had half an hour to spare before another appointment in Whitehall, decided to turn the short distance into a brisk constitutional through St James' Park.

So it was that he found himself brought up short behind the dawdling Nora Clegg, and hemmed in on either side by tourists, at the approach to Bird Cage corner. The traffic hurtled round like a viciously spinning top. Fuming, he spotted a gap in the maelstrom, and swinging his briefcase with annoyance, shoved past Nora and lunged towards the road. The briefcase, catching under the handle of Nora Clegg's bag, dragged her in his wake. Straight into the path of a careering taxi. Tyres screeched. Someone screamed.

"Look. It was a bizarre accident. My briefcase caught . . . Where's my briefcase?" He was trembling. "Look, I'm sorry. I've got to get to an important meeting." He kept looking at his watch.

The briefcase had been sliced in half.

The ambulance came and went. He was prodded and questioned and made to sit down. He could recall an old woman lying crumpled in the road. A young taxi driver, his face chalk white. A big ugly handbag on the ground with breadcrumbs spilling out of it. One shoe. A beige hat with a little pheasant feather in it. He remembered a mass of gaping faces, a few tourists surreptitiously taking pictures.

He had no recollection whatever of how he came to be at the hospital. It seemed to be several hours later. He was aware of people speaking to him. Questions. Hot drinks. He was aware at one point that his teeth were chattering. He heard murmuring voices.

Mechanically he swallowed some pills. "Have they got my briefcase?" he heard himself say. "I've got to have my briefcase."

"Would you like to see her?" A crisp female face floated into his vision. Someone took his arm. He heard the voice telling him that he couldn't stay very long "I'll come back for you in a little while." He heard the door close.

Slowly, the room seemed to coalesce, settle itself into recognizable forms. Michael Bateson could not have said how many beds were in it. The only bed he saw was Nora's. She looked pitifully small. He thought of a fallen sparrow. Her face, drained of colour against the white sheet and pillow, reflected a faint greenish tinge.

He moved closer, sat down in the chair next to the bed. She did not open her eyes. He saw the battered handbag standing on a bedside table. The handle had been wrenched off. It reminded him of a bulldog that had just been in a fight.

Michael Bateson had seen accidents before. He had strolled away from them without a qualm. And once, a car, coming down the ramp of a feed road had suddenly careened out of control and smashed head-on into a cement lamp standard, right in front of him. He had had time to see a woman behind the wheel and a child of three or four in the passenger seat. Both disappeared on impact. He had not stopped. It would have made him late. In the mirror he saw other cars stop and people racing to the crash. Somebody else could handle it.

Unbidden, that scene re-enacted itself before him now. He felt bewildered. Something astonishing seemed to be happening to him. His shoulders shook. He found he could not see. Water seemed to be pouring down the walls of the room wherever he looked—his fingers, the edge of the bed. He heard a sound like a farm animal in pain, and knew it to be himself.

At that moment, the crystal bubble that insulated Michael Bateson shattered at last.

"Micky?"

He froze with shock. "Micky, are you there?" The voice was scarcely audible, but there could be no question that that was what she had said. Her eyes were still closed.

"Micky?"

"Y . . . yes?"

"Mustn't fret."

"What?"

"Got to go sometime, duck." There was a pause. "Micky?"

"Er . . . Yes?"

"Old Ginger 'ad a go at me dinner yesdy."

"Yes?"

"Micky? Can you see me bag? Got something for you. Not much, now." The voice trailed away. He could hear his own heartbeat. "Get it for me will you duck?"

Obediently, he rose and reached for the bag.

"Just a bar of chocolate. For being a good boy."

He opened the bag and rummaged. A battered purse, some keys with a key ring that said 'A Present from Majorca', a concertina wallet filled with snaps, mostly of a child with some furry animals, crumbs everywhere, a picture of the Queen, a comb, a little bottle of lavender water. The Bounty Bar was at the bottom. He retrieved it and restored the bag to its place. It scowled at him.

"Got it?"

"Yes."

"What do you say?"

"Yes. Thank you."

"Good. Want a bit of a snooze now. Blummin legs 'urt. Come back tomorrow, lovie, if I ain't wearin' me 'alo."

"Yes. Yes, I will."

She said nothing more. Michael Bateson stared at the bar of chocolate. He took a deep breath. It was confusing. He was distraught, but at the same time suddenly calm. He felt wretched but somehow valiant as well. Flawed, yet gleaming, like a pebble after rain. The calamity had been his own doing. It appalled him. Yet he had felt the arid years fall away from him like a husk.

He looked down at his unlikely messiah, leaned over and kissed her lightly on the forehead. "You must get well, Nora. You must. Must!" He squeezed her hand.

The nurse returned. It's Micky," he told her. I'll be back tomorrow.

*   *   *

p.m.

He caught a late train home. He'd waited in order to check on Nora. "Stable," they said. She was rallying. The sister said she was a tough old bird.

He sat in the carriage and gazed out of the window with a new awareness. And a new curiosity. He caught sight of his own faint reflection, no longer contained by the sooty pane but framed against a moving tableau of trees, houses, sky. A sky he hadn't looked at in thirty years. He took off his tie. He stretched. Then he opened the new briefcase he had bought. It was empty, apart from Nora's Bounty bar.

He stared at it, wondering who the Micky was it had been intended for. But then, he was Micky, too. Perhaps it had been intended for him all along?

Thoughtfully he tore open the wrapper and began to munch. He had the sensation that he had been given a lifeline, as if the chocolate bar were a baton in some unfathomable relay race. He was about to polish off the second segment when he had an idea. The train drubbed to a halt. It was his stop. He smiled. Carefully, he laid the Bounty bar back in its wrapper and set it on the window ledge.

*   *   *

Adelaide looked down at the wrapper in her hand. Something odd was happening to her breathing. Her whole being, poised on the edge of a great stillness, felt suddenly enveloped in renewal, the pledge of a distant embrace. Exhilaration surged through her and erupted in a riotous shout of joy.

The untouched half of a Bounty Bar lay in her outstretched palm.

"Come on, Sunny! Sing!"

MADELEINE TIME

I'd been daydreaming as usual. But then I noticed it was gone. You'd think someone else might have noticed as well, wouldn't you? People just don't care! I mean it's hard to lose a baby on a bus! At least, I assume that was where I left it. Somebody had probably sat on it by now.

The bus hadn't been crowded. That was the problem. No need for me to sit there clutching Jemima. I probably dumped her on the seat and just forgot. I left my Auntie's dachshund in the loo at Peterborough station once. I didn't remember until somebody raced down the platform babbling that a nasty dog had been lying in wait behind the lavatory bowl, and a retired postmistress's underwear had been slashed to ribbons. Terrible!

"You're just not thinking, Madeleine!"

I am, though. I'm busy studying. People, that is. I have a rich fantasy life. I try to assign them to a time in history that fits. I study their clothes, their features, the way they carry themselves. It's not only my hobby. It's my job. Well, it would be if I could corner some buyers. I design clothes, you see. Unusual clothes. What I want to do is popularise historical costume!

Imagine going to a Parents' Evening in a Roman toga! Simple, elegant. Understated. Or out to dinner in an Elizabethan ruff and cloak. (With gown, of course!) Even more exciting, picture your husband or boyfriend or lover – or all three, if you've struck it lucky – resplendent as King Arthur, or a sheikh, or, if you can stand the ecstasy, a gladiator! No more boring commuter uniforms. They'd all be free to express themselves openly, without having to resort to boxer shorts saying "Rule Britannia!" under the charcoal greys, or those red briefs with a female hand silk-screened on the strategic area. Think what it would do for the Balance of Trade. I am launching a fashion idea whose time has definitely come!

For the moment, though, I have to pay the rent, buy my fabrics and feed my cat. So I freelance as an assistant wardrobe mistress. Currently, I'm with a theatre in the West End. Which means I have to commute. Which brings me back to Jemima.

Commuters, by the way, are ideal subjects for assessment. They're all trapped. That chap, for instance, with the fair hair, strong face and stocky build. He was made for the Philadelphia of 1776. And that patrician woman with the hawk nose and commendable posture could discard her Burberry raincoat to advantage in favour of Aztec robes and plumage! As for the tall, young, arrogant, darkly brooding, broad-shouldered etc. etc. strap-hanger opposite: what a splendid Regency buck he would make in a high collared coat, waterfall cravat, polished Hessian boots, and those deliriously tight pantaloons!

I sit across the aisle, appraising him with utter sartorial satisfaction. He catches my eye. His gaze hovers a moment, registers a mild, condescending interest, drops to the bundle of joy in my lap, returns with a contemptuous sneer to my two-timing Jezebel face, and with a flick of his Mr Darcy shoulders, focuses on the middle distance.

I continue my appraisal. He begins to fidget with his watch. He runs a hand through his hair just as the train gives a lurch and almost loses his balance. I find my gaze thoughtfully returning to his thighs. The Regency buck, you know, must have the superb thighs of a Colin Firth, a Matthew Macfadyen or an Aidan Turner. It's absolutely critical!

I try to gauge the necessary suppleness and muscle tone under his pin stripes. Absently glancing at his face, I am just in time to witness his nonchalant indifference dissolve under a flush as scarlet as a boiled prawn.

Oh dear! Have I made him feel like a sex object? I really must make an effort to be more considerate whenever my obsession intrudes. "Madeleine, you're just not thinking!"

(Anyway, he wouldn't have made much of a Roman. No aplomb!)

Speaking of men, you're wondering about Jemima again, aren't you? Well, she's not actually mine. I mean, I'm not married. Or . . . er . . . unmarried, if you understand what I mean.

You see, one morning, as I stood, or rather was propped vertically in a heaving mass of inhumanity on the tube, I decided, as I removed an elbow from my left eye, felt a rucksack obliterate my feet, and took out my snorkel, that there had to be a better way to beat the odds against nabbing a seat.

"What," I said to myself, as I lunged out of my scrum for a suddenly vacant strap, in competition with a good contestant for the role of Attila the Hun, "What," I said again, as I limped back to my huddle near the door, "would budge that complacent city type reading his *Independent*, dislodge that Japanese tourist's grin (and his camera), and bring them both leaping to their chivalrous feet?"

That day, I recall, was a Princess of Troy day. I pushed my golden headband—an old necklace hung with golden balls and triangles—higher on my forehead, like Indiana Jones shoving up his hat, to think with an uncluttered brain. Alas! Not a flicker.

At Holborn, I made another lunge. My headband slipped to my nose, and my heel jammed in the floor grooves. So I missed it again. It was like being an eternal bridesmaid. The whole business was assuming emotional proportions.

But as we pulled into Leicester Square, the light bulb finally, blindingly, snapped on. The solution, so simple, had dawned before you could say "Mind the gap!"

Back at the theatre, I ransacked the props room and emerged, half an hour later, with a lace tablecloth, a doll and a rattle. A bit of clever swathing and I had what I hoped would be my fool proof, portable seat reservation. I adjusted my features to an expression of stoical and pathetic resignation. "So, Jemima," I crooned, one cunning eye on the mirror, "it's you and me against the world, kid!"

On the tube next day, it was harder work than I'd thought. After all, people don't really look at each other much, do they? I cooed dispiritedly, waving the rattle. I whimpered with fright at every lurch of the carriage. No response. I decided to sway alarmingly. Success! A schoolboy jumped up to steady me, and bingo, three assorted men leapt to their feet!

"Mustn't forget, now," I told myself, as I sank with appropriate, thankful exhaustion into a seat. "Mustn't go and muck it up by absentmindedly stuffing the lot into the oversized bag I use for fabrics." So I concentrated, closed my eyes, and thought of historical England.

The plan, then, was a good one. But nothing, it seems, is truly fool proof. Probably because there are such ingenious fools, like me. After all, scarcely three months later I left Jemima, you will recall, on a sparsely populated bus!

It was hardly surprising, really, after the day I'd had. A matinee day. And a costume disaster! Rips, safety pins (four tins), spray paint, and aspirins. Even a swim at the health club round the corner hadn't changed my impression that somebody's derangement --probably mine--was imminent.

And, of course, later, as it was my evening off, I obeyed the forlorn compulsion to visit a certain supermarket again. As always, it was fruitless. Well, there was fruit. But you know what I mean.

No . . ! You *don't* know about all that, do you!

You see, as I'm sure you've suspected, I've been yearning to meet a consul--the ideal Roman, that is! (And I don't mean Pontius Pilate.) There is something irresistible about a clued-up, in-charge Roman with the features of Chris Hemsworth, or Gerard Butler with a twinkle in his eye; something compelling about his mental intensity as he grapples with empires; something unnerving about the suggestion of tanned limbs under the regal nonchalance of his toga.

Then, one Wednesday, there he was, studying the biscuit shelf at Sainsbury's.

From his expression, he could have been planning the invasion of Gaul. Or even to divide it into three parts!

Blood thundered in my temples. I dropped the tin of sardines poised in my hand. Oblivious, he turned to contemplate the Bourbon creams. I was beside myself. Mentally, I removed his sport's shirt and jeans, and draped his athletic form in the elegant folds of a white toga bordered with blue. He might have stepped from the set of *Rome.* My knees trembled.

He turned. We stood face to face. I attempted to smile. His grey eyes widened. His brow creased in bewilderment. "Good. Isn't vain," I thought. "Doesn't imagine women are chasing him all over supermarkets." His gaze took in my modest Egyptian headdress (thank God I hadn't decided to be a Russian peasant that day!), and to my disgust, my face began to flame. (Oh, the fiddling I had in mind if Rome burned!)

He twinkled. In fact, his mouth unmistakeably twitched. Then he smiled. Truly smiled. It was almost a smile of . . . appreciation?

He was almost at the checkout. I had to hear his voice. Just in case (I shuddered) he turned into Peewee Herman. I needn't have worried. With the resonant tones of "Did you double-bag the tomatoes?" my fate was sealed, the die was cast, my Rubicon crossed. But by the time I managed to get out of my stupor and out of the store, he was gone.

After that, I haunted Sainsbury's of course.

I didn't see him again for weeks. When I did, it wasn't in the supermarket. It was in the worst of all possible places. The tube! With Jemima!

I remember the seat being offered. But the grateful simper died on my lips. Rome was looking down at me with astonishment. His gaze shifted from me to Jemima with—did I imagine it?—a wince of dismay. He smiled politely, and withdrew. Five minutes later, he disappeared into the fray at Charing Cross. And of course I would be in my Russian peasant gear!

So here I stood, a month later, pondering these matters, while Jemima and the bus roared into oblivion.

"Hang on, though," I thought. "Wait a minute!" Something seemed to be nibbling at my mind. I shoved up my Pocahontas headband. Of course! I didn't leave Jemima on the bus at all. Now I remembered!

I'd bunged her into a spare locker at the swimming pool! No Jemima tomorrow, no seat. I raced back to the club.

As I yanked Jemima out of the locker in triumph, a middle-aged woman, aghast, fled shrieking towards the lobby. She gibbered at the receptionist, pointing. I brandished Jemima and tossed her into the air. The bundle flurried to the floor.

"See!" I cried. "Not even a whimper!"

"It's vile!" she screeched.

"It's plastic," I hissed, smiling wickedly.

One hand clutching her throat, the woman backed into the street.

Turning, I saw that someone else was watching me with patent amusement. He was leaning against a pillar, a gym bag over his shoulder and books under his arm. I thought I must be hallucinating on chlorine. But then again, where would you expect to find a Roman but at the baths?

Solemnly, he picked up Jemima and offered her to me upside-down.

"Yours, I believe," he said gravely.

He dropped one of his books. I retrieved it.

"Yours, I believe?" I countered, smiling nervously. I paused. "Is it . . . er . . . a good read?"

"Well *I* think so," he replied, twinkling. "It's my field."

My pulse raced. "What's your field?"

"Oh," he chuckled, "I don't think you'd care too much for that." He moved closer. "But then, again, you might." He looked down quizzically into my face. "The Fall of the Roman Empire!"

FINN

The swan's long neck shot out like a snake. The boy stood his ground. The swan reared, flapping its massive wingspan, then lunged, hissing viciously at the boy's elbow. Calmly, still clutching the little bag of crumbs, he raised it out of harm's way. His composure unsettled the bird. It held his gaze, glaring beadily, unsure whether to subside or attack. The boy flung his breadcrumbs in a half disappointed, half contemptuous gesture. Then, with a defiant toss of his head, he turned and sauntered down the towpath. Was he going to look back, just in case the bird …? Not a chance! The boy had a fierce dignity that regardless of the absence or presence of witnesses, he always strove to maintain. It gave him a sense of control over his haphazard existence. It put a bit of a shine on it, a little swoosh of lah-de-dah.

That was his Ma's expression: "lah-de-dah". His grave expression flickered at the recollection. She was all right, was Ma, except for this one thing that seemed to get under her skin. She would sharpen the rebuke like a weapon, hurling it at him when he least expected. But it never pierced his heart. *Nah! Not me!*

He wandered towards a moored barge--a handsome canal boat, complete with blue spotted curtains and a row of terracotta pots overflowing with geraniums and pansies on the roof. It lay placidly on the silver sheen of the canal. The boy found the stillness of the water hypnotic. It could entice you to fall asleep staring into its depths. You could fall in. But you would come up laughing, shaking little diamonds out of your hair.

He leaned against the mooring post, his hands in his pockets, and turned his attention to a willow trailing languid fingers above the keel. Lithe shadows bobbed and dipped in time with it on the bright blue paint. Entranced, his mind groped towards something he couldn't quite reach. It made him feel suddenly bereft.

He jumped as frantic barking erupted behind him. The mortified swan was having a go at the next unfortunate who came too close to its territory. The yapping stopped abruptly. Several seconds of uneasy quiet followed. They were shattered by a screech. A Jack Russell, teeth bared, eyes bulging, shot up the towpath, veered through a gap in the hedge and disappeared into an adjacent field. "Henry!" A hefty woman in muddy joggers and a denim jacket tried to sprint after him brandishing the lead, but could only manage an uncomfortable lope. "Henry!" She blustered past the boy, who paid her no attention. Her voice dwindled as she, too, blundered into the field and disappeared.

The boy grinned to himself. Jack Russells were supposed to be feisty. Why didn't the little tosser stand and fight? He liked to see somebody hold their nerve. Somebody ought to write to the Queen. After all, the swans belonged to Her Maj. Or so he'd been told. It must be … he groped for an appropriate word …'barongo', no, 'megabarongo' to own all the swans in England. He smiled to himself. You could eat the buggers at Christmas.

He sighed. Time to get back. He sauntered down the towpath. As he reached the curve, he turned and stood very still, looking back at the barge. He appraised the composition it presented, framed by the water and the sky. Again, that odd sensation of disappointment, of something that seemed to elude him.

"Hey, gypo!" His head snapped round. A clatch of younger boys stood watching him, blocking the towpath. Every face registered unpleasant anticipation. It was their leader who had spoken, a heavy-faced boy at the front with his arms folded. Behind him, a fair-haired boy with an incongruously angelic face put in his oar. "You tell him, Trev!"

Trev taunted again: "Hey, pikey! Yeah, you!"

The gypsy boy raised his eyebrows and stared at them, exasperated. *No peace anywhere. No quiet.* He inclined his head in a mocking gesture of defeat. Then he held up his arms in an ok-you-win gesture, turned and ambled back the way he had come. The boys, in commando mode, crept along behind him, hugging the hedge. The fair-haired angel rushed up and hurled a handful of gravel from the path at the back of his head. "Dirty little pikey!"

He kept on walking.

In daring little sallies, two or three more rushed up and did the same. The boy stopped, squared his shoulders. *Enough.* As the next aspiring hero crept up, he shot round, grabbed him by the wrist with his left hand and landed a hard right in the boy's face. He fell, groaning. The gypsy boy bent and shoved the boy's hand, still filled with gravel, down inside his T-shirt. Then he punched the hand. The boy yelped.

"Anybody else?" The boy had a faint Irish accent.

The gang stayed silent. The injured boy scrambled to his feet and backed away, his nose bloody. Trev stepped forward, fist clenched. "You pikeys are nothin' but trouble." There were catcalls of agreement. His voice rose to a yell. "You should be deported!" The gang advanced slowly, closing in. They were now almost level with the barge. Trev moved to one side. "Get 'im!" The youngest boy, determined to impress him, lobbed a ball of dried horse manure at the silent young gypsy. It missed and landed on the barge. Trev was turning to cuff him when the rest of the group stopped dead.

A young woman of about thirty, and of mixed race, had materialized in front of them. She was wearing a blue dress, a matching head band over thick brown hair and a fierce expression. She was also brandishing a broom. "Clear off, you little trouble makers, or . . . " she paused ominously as her stare swept from face to face ". . . I'll set Charlie on you!"

"Who's Charlie, then, your chihuahua?" The 14-year old Trev postured defiance as he stuck out his lower lip, displaying a bit of un-chewed crisp.

She spoke quietly with a lilting accent, but there was no mistaking her tone: ". . . he'll take a piece out of your bum before you can say 'bad-tempered swan'."

"Swan?" They stared at her.

"That swan is a bastard!" They craned to look behind her. The gypsy boy was smiling wickedly. "Just saw him kill a cat."

They looked about nervously, clustering against the hedge. "Where's the swan, Trev?" piped the youngest, who was eleven. "Where is it?"

"Here, Charlie!" The gypsy boy was going with the flow. His voice rose. "Charleee . . . Fresh bums to bite!"

"You're a no-good pikey!" It was the youngest boy, again. Trev clapped the lad approvingly on the back.

"'S right. He needs a lesson, and we're gonna give it to him."

"Clear off, all of you!" The woman advanced a few steps and raised the broom as if she was about to pole vault.

"I can take care of myself!" It was the gypsy boy. His eyes glittered. "Leave off!"

The woman eyed him contemptuously. "Scum." She turned back to the gang. "And that goes for you lot as well!"

Trev folded his arms again. Several other boys instantly copied him. "We ent scared of no . . ." He cast about for a suitable insult and failed. "Where's this swan, then?" The question hung in the air. "Can't scare us," blustered another boy.

The woman smiled and raised her voice. "Charlie!" She banged the end of her broom on the ground twice. "Charleee . . . !" The huge swan emerged from behind the barge in a flurry of wings. He paused, neck swaying, beak open, eyes fixed in fury--an avenging angel. *Whose bum to go for?*

Brandishing her broom like Boudicca leading an assault, the woman pointed it at the boys: "At 'em, birdie!" Charlie reared and lunged.

They scattered in disarray, yelling. A few crashed through the hedge. The others, including Trev, tore off down the towpath. The youngest, left behind, tried to dive through the hedge further up. There was no gap. In panic, yelping at the thorns, he thrashed through and disappeared.

The enraged swan flounced back and glared at the gypsy boy, who had not moved. "Bunk off birdie!" The two faced each other down.

"And you can bunk off as well," the woman added. "Ungrateful little no-good . . ." She jabbed at him with the broom. He stood his ground.

"Leave off!"

"Shall I set Charlie on you as well?"

"Suit yourself."

The swan hissed. The boy stood motionless.

"Now then, Rita, don't include him!" The voice, gravelly with age, suggested laid-back amusement. He turned to see a small woman in candy pink dungarees that were too big for her regarding him from the deck of the blue barge. "Well done, boy! You can stand up for yourself I see."

He stared at her, unsure whether he was being praised or slyly ridiculed.

She waved a potted geranium. "Not a brawler, are you? And you can think on your feet. I do like that."

He had an acute ear for sarcasm, but detected none in her tone. He stared at her mutely, his apparent power to think on his feet deserting him. He tried to make out her face. It was hidden by the most extravagant hat the boy had ever seen. It was a cream confection festooned with chiffon and net, clearly more suitable for a society wedding. He straightened. "Yeah, well my Ma wouldn't agree with you, missus."

"Ma'am."

"What?"

"Ma'am."

"Oh, er . . ." He paused, found his voice and grinned. "Aye do beg your pardon!" He swept into an exaggerated bow, carefully positioning his backside away from the swan. "Milady."

The swan hissed and reared. Rita almost reared as well. "Cheeky little . . ."

The old woman laughed. Her laugh was young. "Rita . . ." The old woman pointed at Charlie. "Please, dear."

Rita scowled, about to protest. There was a short pause. She shrugged, tutted, stepped forward and hand-gestured "down" to Charlie, who instantly subsided. He craned his neck up at her and waited for any further instructions.

"Thank you, dear." Depositing the plant with care among the riot of flowers on the roof, the old woman turned to the boy. "Ever been on a barge?"

"Nah."

This was too much for Rita. Scoffing, she sidled off down the towpath towards a green and yellow houseboat, the broom balanced over her shoulder. Charlie waddled meekly after her, like a distracted puppy. She threw him something from her pocket. He gobbled it and looked at her expectantly. She clapped her hands and shooed him. "Bye-bye Charlie." At once he flapped to the edge of the canal and settled, with great dignity, onto the water beside the boat.

The young gypsy stared after her.

"You look disgruntled, boy." The old woman was addressing him. He tried not to look puzzled. *Disgruntled?*

"Browned off?" she added helpfully. He bridled. She laughed again. Then she flung her head back and her arms wide as if to encompass the sky, the trees, the canal in an affirmation of delight. Who could be browned off on a day like this?

Bonkers, he thought. *Daft biddy.*

"Come and have a cup of my special brew."

"Gotta get home. My sister'll nag my head off, missus."

"Don't you like tea? And it's ma'am."

"Yeah, yeah." She didn't look like an axe murderer or an abductor of truculent young nobodies who stood up for themselves. With what he hoped was an air of insolent ennui, he strolled aboard. He was curious.

"There, you see. Now you've been on a barge." She indicated two little cushioned chairs crammed in the stern and flopped down with a sigh of contentment. He could smell the sharp tang of geraniums and under it the sweetness of pansies.

"Don't just stand there gawping. Sit."

"I'm not a dog."

She chuckled. "Got a bark, though, haven't you!"

"Huh." He stalked over and sat down.

"Good. Now what shall I call you? Swan boy?"

He wondered if she'd seen his earlier encounter with the bad-tempered bird. *Good.*

"Mr. Cool?" she went on.

He managed a slight smile.

"Or . . ." She appeared to be thinking hard. "What was it? Pikey?"

He refused to be drawn. "Can't help how I was born."

"No indeed." She nodded approvingly.

There was a silence.

"Well?"

"Well what?"

"What's your name?" she chided softly, and grinned. She waited.

He gave in. "It's Vanslow." He paused. Vanslow Fion Buckingham."

"Like the palace."

"Yeah, like the palace."

She studied him. He stared back. "So . . . what should I call you?"

A ghost of a smile. He looked out over the water. "Finn."

"Ah, like Finn McCool!"

He grinned. "That's the one."

"Pleased to meet you, Finn. I'm May."

She removed the lavish hat and tossed it on a stool. She stretched and looked up at the cloudless sky. He studied her face. It was papery pale, with a patchwork tracery of lines so fine that from a distance they would have been invisible. Her lips, though thin with age, had an amiable upward curve. But it was her eyes, the colour of faded blue denim that held his gaze. He thought of an uncertain spring sky. But there was nothing uncertain about their expression. They were full of life, arrestingly bright. *Sunlit water*. Her hair was pure white, short, softly waved. A few wisps rose and fell in the warm breeze.

"Thought you asked me if I wanted a cup of tea?"

She chuckled. "You didn't give me an answer." She got up. He noted that she showed none of the discomfort he had observed on the faces of older people getting out of chairs. She went lightly down some steps into the barge interior. Minutes passed. A blue spotted curtain jigged. Her head popped out of the window. "Well, are you coming or not? This is not a millionaire's yacht, you know. There aren't any white-gloved waiters. You'll have to just pig it."

Then he did smile broadly. *Feisty cow*. He sauntered down the steps. On the last one, he found himself gaping open-mouthed at the ordered little sitting room. There was a mini-bureau, a blue sofa with a pattern of white wisteria, and a compact, easy chair to match. A marble mermaid, arms raised, held up a circle of glass beside it. He was used to confined spaces, but this was far more pleasant than the cramped wagons and mobile homes he had known ever since he could remember.

"Sit where you like. Kettle's boiling." She retreated into a neat but narrow kitchen. He heard the clink of crockery, followed by a clatter. "Bugger!"

He grinned. She was all right, was Ma'am.

"Rita!" He heard her knock the window. "Tea?" Moments later, the woman in the blue dress appeared in the doorway, minus her broom. Her lip curled at the sight of the boy lounging on the sofa.

"What's *he* . . . ?"

"Rita." The firm tone implied no argument. "Sit down and talk to him, dear girl. I'll be there in a minute."

Rita glared at the boy and stalked over to the easy chair. She flicked her dress, sat down. Silence. She began tapping her fingers on the arms of the chair. The boy watched her, amused. She turned her head and looked at him with disdain. He raised an eyebrow. This annoyed her even more. She turned away. He examined her profile with interest.

"You're crazy, May."

"No need to shout, dear." There was another clatter in the kitchen, followed by a muttered oath.

"Well you are!" Rita stared pointedly at the boy and called again. "Another stray dog!"

He looked at her, his face expressionless. "I'm not a stray dog." His tone was self-assured, rather than petulant.

May's response from the kitchen was a whoop of triumph. "Woooof!"

She emerged with a tray and three china mugs, which she set carefully over the marble mermaid. A little plate of biscuits nestled in the middle. Rita got up at once and selected a mug. The boy looked on. She scowled at him as she resumed her seat. May, too, gave him a look. "Go on, boy. Pig it."

"Delighted . . . *Ma'am*," he replied gravely. A few seconds of silence. "And it's *Finn*." He leaned over, picked up a mug and sank back on the comfortable sofa. May's lips twitched. He sipped appreciatively. "And this is Marguerite," said May. He made a face. "It's the long version of Rita." She took the last mug and sat down beside him.

A few more swallows and he was on his feet again. He offered her the plate of biscuits, ignoring Rita. May tried, with only partial success, to stifle her amusement.

"So, Finn," she said, looking at him steadily. "Why don't you tell us about those spray cans!"

*   *   *

Spray cans? That was two weeks ago, further up the canal.

He'd done it at night, *so how . . . ? Was the old girl an owl, or what?*

He had been charging down a field that afternoon with an angry farm hand and a stable boy in hot pursuit. He didn't think they had much hope of catching him. He was riding a frisky bay mare at the gallop. It was the sensation of trotting that he had wanted. It reminded him of . . . But discovery provoked the sudden need for speed. So he was going full tilt.

He looked behind him. His pursuers were barely into the field. He veered through a gap leading into a second field. Time to choose discretion. Sometimes it was the better part of foolhardy. He negotiated the animal into a circle and threw himself off the horse—easy when you're riding bareback. He slapped its hind quarters. The horse kicked up her heels and galloped on.

He thought he would get away with it. The boy knew all his pursuers wanted was to get the horse back. *Holy Mother! I only wanted a ride.* He scrambled through a thorny gap in the hedge and found himself on a towpath, next to the canal.

Responding, as always, to the soothing proximity of water, he decided on a stroll. But he was unprepared for what came next. He stopped, open-mouthed. The hedge had given way to a long, concrete wall. To be more accurate, the wall formed the back of a series of farm buildings. It continued as far as a paddock further along, where the hedge re-appeared.

The wall was covered with graffiti. Most of them were obscene. Some were in jumbo block letters trumpeting somebody's contempt for Frankie, that slapper Midge, hearts stabbed by arrows, and other such broadcasts to the community of ducks and serene canal traffic. The messages and pictures were in lurid yellows, reds and smudged black, like soot.

The wall offended his sensibilities, but he found himself assessing it. He sauntered along it, hands behind his back, like a visitor at an art gallery. Beneath the disgust, there it was again, that strange, clenching sensation, that feeling of having lost something before he even knew he had it.

He found that he was angry.

That evening he came back, armed with spray cans retrieved from the community cache for touch ups and signs at the caravan site. He had chosen white. Lots of white. He waited for nightfall and set to work. There was a moon, ensuring reflected light from the water. He could see enough to do the job. The cool tang of the canal and of green growing things disappeared under a miasma of paint fumes that made him cough. But he persisted. He felt driven. An hour later he stood back in satisfaction at his handiwork. He had sprayed over a particularly offensive group of pictures. Twice. Coverage was complete. Before him was a section of pristine, white wall. He imagined it heaving a sigh of relief. He had ridded it of the insults it had suffered. He could identify with that.

He stared at it. Again, that odd feeling.

He got home after midnight. A dog barked. More joined in. "And what have you been up to?" His brother-in-law, Declan, responding to the knock, stood with his hands on his hips in his pyjama bottoms on the top step of the caravan. "What's up with you, boyo?" The boy raised his chin defiantly and said nothing. But the smudge of paint on his face told a tale. "Paint? Why can't you paint the hen coop, Finn? You can be a useless waste of space, that you can." He cuffed him round the ear. "The way we live, space is important! Get in with you!"

*   *   *

May was still looking at him expectantly.

"Well?"

"You're always saying that."

"I was moored on the other side of the canal. Couldn't sleep. I came out on deck and saw you."

He felt, rather than saw, Rita's expression change. He stared at the floor.

"Amazing!"

He looked up. May was smiling. She threw up her arms. "You should have seen it, Rita. In the middle of all that graffiti rubbish . . ."

"Yes," murmured Rita. "You said. A number of times."

May barrelled on, her voice rising with enthusiasm. ". . . a trotting, piebald horse, mane flying. Life-sized." She paused and flopped back, her eyes closed. "Beautifully done, especially considering the restrictions he had to work with. If he'd had proper brushes and all, who knows?"

He blinked. Something swelled up in his throat and threatened to choke him. *What do I say?*

They were both looking at him. "Just mucking about," he managed. "Couldn't leave it blank, could I?" He rushed on. "Thought it looked like a canvas, all white and . . . . Well I . . . It . . Thought I'd have a go. Wasn't too bad."

"It looked like a labour of love to me."

He flushed. "Nah." He didn't know where to look. Rita was staring at him with an odd expression.

"You must have a startling memory," May went on, "because you weren't copying it from anything, were you?"

He found himself tongue-tied.

" . . . And the way he was working." She turned to Rita. "So . . . so . . . intense."

"So what is it about you and horses?" It was Rita, her grudging tone failing to conceal her curiosity.

Finn stood up, stuffed his hands in his pockets. "I'd better be off."

"Come on," coaxed May. "Our young man of mystery. Aren't you going to tell us."

"Nothing to tell." He hesitated, then sat down again. He leaned forward, his hands between his knees, head down, staring at the carpet. "I like 'em, that's all."

"Horses," said Rita. There was a softer note to her voice.

"Horses."

*   *   *

Ma and Da lived in the heart of the travellers' community in the west of Ireland. They had a mobile home and a traditional caravan, the sort that old fashioned pictures always classified as "typically gypsy", rounded like a prairie wagon, clanking with gleaming copperware, painted in bright colours and designs of flowers, and drawn by a horse, sometimes two, with another two tethered behind. So did everyone else of their acquaintance. They would journey from horse fair to horse fair, visiting relatives, competing in the endless trotting races, selling and buying their horses in canny trading, where a wink and a handshake were usually enough to clinch a deal (until they changed the rules at Ballinasloe, where every sale had to be registered). Da was a bare-knuckle fighter and always drew a crowd. They would marvel at his prowess, bet, and wonder slyly if they were going to witness the drama of his defeat. So far, he had reigned supreme.

It was hard to go to school in such circumstances. And this was what irked the boy. His older sisters were content to travel and absorb themselves in the family's vast social network. They were cheerfully husband-hunting. Pretty girls with eye-catching figures, they could afford to be choosy and take their time. His younger brother, Reese, wanted to be a fighter like his Da.

But Finn was different. Lah-de-dah. Odd. He wanted to read. He wanted to learn. To discover the great unknown territories of literature and history. He wanted to speak unaccented English. What saved him from being a total misfit was his love of horses. He had an obvious affinity with them. They took to him. They trotted like the devil for him as he sat in the racing buggy with barely any pressure on the reins. They seemed to know instinctively what he wanted them to do. He won lots of races, pleased a lot of people and was as happy as he was able in their company.

And then his sister, Kath, met Declan, the man of her dreams, and got engaged. After the wedding they were planning to cross to England to see some of their English relatives, go up to the Appleby Fair and, well, do the rounds. The urge to widen his horizons was irresistible to Finn.

"Can I come as well?"

His other sister, Lacey, cuffed him. "Sure you can't expect to be crowdin' them in their first year together, you daft thing."

The wedding went off with all the overkill extravagance of such milestones in the traveller community. Relatives came from all over county Galway. It was a noisy, lavish affair. The bride's dress was too wide for her to walk properly up the aisle. Something it had not occurred to them to anticipate. Her father had to escort her to the altar sideways. Her train, fifteen feet of glittering white tulle, had to be lifted over the pews and above the heads of the guests by the bridesmaid and three of the tallest female guests from the congregation. The wedding cake drew into the reception in a silver-coloured racing buggy with metal, life-sized horses.

Finn enjoyed the food but soon tired of the noise and crush. Two girls, his cousins several times removed, each dragged him onto the dance floor and gave him melting looks. One tried to drag him off to a room behind the hotel kitchens. He'd had a few beers—allowed on this occasion—which had gone to his head, and he wondered if they would get away with a bit of a snog. He was almost fifteen, after all. Nearly a man. The girl was pretty and inviting. But when, in no uncertain terms, she wanted him to go further, he suddenly balked and slammed out of the room, affronted by her matter-of-fact forwardness. Colourful abuse rang in his ears.

He found himself looking for a bit of peace in the hotel residents' lounge, which was empty. To his delight, it had a small library.

The boy did not own a book. They took up space. They were considered unnecessary to the travelling lifestyle, where living was not meant to be vicarious, but immediate. The family had a bible, of course, and a missal. But that was all. He had tried to join local libraries, but none would accept his lack of a fixed address.

Now he found himself facing three shelves of real books and no one to tell him not to touch. He examined the tooled leather bindings with wonder. Oscar Wilde was here. George Bernard Shaw. Joyce. Lord Tennyson. Shelley. Philip Larkin. Walt Whitman. Shakespeare. He pulled down "Hamlet" but could make little sense of it. The Elizabethan verse and unfamiliar phrasings were too much of a struggle. "A Treasury of Irish Poets", bound in red, attracted his attention. Better. He sank into a leather chair and began to read. A delicious feeling of rightness, of comfort, stole over him. He felt at home. Did you have to understand poetry, or could you just feel it?

He turned a page and was instantly entranced by Yeats. "The Song of Wandering Aengus" seemed to be speaking directly to him—to the fire in his own head, to all his thwarted, half-felt aspirations, like the little silver trout that turned into a glimmering, eternally elusive girl. It spoke to his heart.

When he was asked, with icy politeness, to leave the residents' lounge "because, young man, you are unfortunately not a hotel resident," he managed to tear out the poem before returning the book to the shelf and stalking out.

It was a year before he managed to get to England. His auntie Kaley and uncle Rick, with their two children (and dog) cheerfully dropped him off at the site where his sister and her husband had decided to stay put until the new baby was a bit older. It was a noisy reunion for all concerned and lasted two days.

Kath and Declan made him welcome, he was family, after all. But he was expected to pull his weight, including babysitting whenever needed. He was used to children, but he found it boring and tedious. And he'd missed the Appleby Fair up in Cumbria. There were no books, of course. And worse, no horses. He was lonely.

On the plus side, at least he had a base now. His sister agreed to enrol him at the local school.

Everybody had been all right to him at first. He was behind in his lessons, that was clear. He had missed so much grounding that he was laughed at for his ignorance. Yet the boy was imaginative and clever in an intuitive way. He was variously described by his teachers as "promising", "keen", and "refreshing", though it was agreed that he clearly balked at discipline.

He found chemistry an enigma. He couldn't decode it at all. Art flummoxed him. Collage, graphics, still life studies of masks and studio oddments? *Why?* He felt a nameless frustration and cut the class.

He'd had a few comments from his peers about his hair. It wasn't green, or shaved, but it was unusual in the non-traveller community. Short on top and at the sides, it flowed in a luxuriant mane from crown to shoulders at the back. It seemed to suggest wildness under control, which enhanced his mystique and drew fascinated glances from girls, startled approval from the boys. That sort of style took some cool.

He was starting to make friends, and for the most part, was doing his best. Until, after less than three weeks, inevitably, his traveller status leaked out. Life instantly became difficult. His attendance dwindled, then stopped altogether. There was the odd, disappointed sigh from two or three female classmates, who had found his quiet but confident reserve intriguing, and agreed he was definitely "fit." Many of the boys made less complimentary remarks. "Good riddance," was particularly popular.

Some members of staff shared a similar opinion. "We don't want his sort here." The snooty art mistress, a Miss Johnson, art connoisseur and something of a fixture on the county art scene, complained that although he had been cutting her class he had been seen hanging about near her studio, "obviously waiting for a chance to purloin something." She added that he had looked menacing. Only the English master, Mr Baker, touched by the boy's eagerness to learn and his delight in reading, as if he'd scarcely seen a book before, was heard to remark quietly: "What a pity."

So there it was. No more school. He haunted the library instead, whenever he could, and read on his own. He also started to help Declan on the construction site.

*   *   *

"We'd like to show you something, Finn," said May. He was still staring mutely at the floor. He looked up. "Wouldn't we, Rita?" May was looking pointedly at the other woman, her eyebrows raised. Rita pretended not to understand. Exasperated, May rose, her face suddenly full of mischief. "I can see you still need convincing. Sit tight." She left them in her little sitting room and went out.

Rita glanced at Finn and then after May. Finn rubbed his face and ran a hand through his hair. *Whatever.* He leaned back. Rita appeared to be thinking. Neither moved.

"What the . . . ?" Finn leapt to his feet. "Where . . . ?" The barge was under way. He rushed on deck. Rita followed. The mulish look on her face, the bewilderment on Finn's, were both met by a laugh from May. "Enjoy, and please, no stupid questions!" Rita looked at her watch.

The barge chugged through a landscape burgeoning into summer. Its serenity entranced Finn. He caught Rita staring at him with ill-concealed distaste. Somehow, he felt too relaxed to care. They reached a water meadow, and beyond it, the bank where, in the middle of the night, May had watched a boy elevate a grotesque piece of concrete into art. This time, she steered towards the bank next to a wall. The painting was still there, untouched except for a scrawl at the bottom in black marker pen: "Baxter is a horse's arse."

"There!" said May. "What have I been telling you?"

"Surprised it's still there," muttered Finn.

Rita stared, wide-eyed. Her mouth had dropped open.

The horse radiated life. The artist had caught its fast, jaunty gait, flaring nostrils, the thrill of the race, though it was not hitched to a buggy. The animal was life-sized and three-quarters on, the foreshortening masterly. He had also captured something else--his own emotional response, his affection, a tender understanding. They were almost tangible.

"And he did it all, can you believe it, with a few coloured spray cans. Bits of rag. He did a lot of fiddling and rubbing, didn't you, Finn?"

Finn stared out at the water, scarlet with embarrassment.

"Well?" said May. "Is he as good as I said?"

Rita looked away. She paused, stared down at her feet and nodded.

May smiled and stood up. She manoeuvred the barge a few yards along the towpath next to a clump of brush and willow.

"Now we wait."

Finn tried to look nonchalant and failed. "What are we waiting for?" No one replied. May raised her hands in a let's-wait-and-see gesture and winked. He bit his lip. *This is getting weird.* He studied his finger nails, fidgeted, watched the ducks.

May produced more tea and biscuits.

Rita looked at her watch again. She drank her tea in silence. But her eyes were far away and intent. They kept flicking back to the horse on the wall.

Nothing happened for almost half an hour.

The quiet was disrupted by an excited black and white border collie as he pranced round the curve in the towpath, all bluster and curiosity. "Jack!" The dog stopped, surveyed the occupants of the barge, then trotted back up the path, a tennis ball firmly clenched in his mouth. Moments later, he re-appeared, skipping round a couple clearly out for a country walk. They balked, grimacing with disgust when they saw the wall. Until they walked a bit further and saw the horse. They stopped dead, staring. In a flurry of excitement, the woman took out her phone and photographed it. They pointed and discussed for several more minutes. The woman saw May and shouted across with delight. "Somebody knows how to paint, eh!" May smiled, made a face and opened her hands wide in the universal gesture of bewilderment.

Jack dropped his ball and barked at the barge, annoyed his walk had been interrupted. Humans were unfathomable. Quivering with impatience, he attempted to round his owners up. He finally succeeded and, tail high, led them off towards beguiling smells further up the canal. The couple waved as they moved off.

Minutes later, a jogger ran past, glancing at the wall. She ran back again as the painting registered and spent a full two minutes staring at it.

Not long after that, a narrow boat chugged by. The occupants, two couples in their twenties, waved. One of the women squeaked excitedly. "Look, John." She pointed at the painting. "There it is! There it is!" One of the men scrambled for an expensive-looking camera and clicked several times. Finn was doing his best to blend into the clump of willows near the bow. The man shouted over to Rita and May. "We saw it on YouTube. Amazing, isn't it?"

"That's what *I* said!" shouted May. The man grinned and raised his upturned thumb. They puttered on, discussing. Finn sat quietly, his face impassive, but May could see the confusion in his eyes.

"*Now* we can go back," she said, smiling across at him. She looked pointedly at Rita. "I rest my case."

*   *   *

May brought the barge back to its original mooring and tied up.

"Gotta go." Finn leapt on to the towpath. She noted he was now openly agitated, though he had said nothing at all on the short return journey. "Hey, thanks and all, ma'am . . ." His tone was deceptively light. " . . . er . . . May. . . er, thanks again." He began to hurry off down the path.

"No, please Finn, wait." shouted May. "Wait! Please!" He stopped. "We've . . ." she glanced at Rita, who was about to disembark. "We've got something to show you. Something important!" She beckoned as if she were deploying an armed incursion. "Come on!" She started off down the towpath.

Finn and Rita looked at each other, sharing a complicit moment of exasperation. Finn's instinct was to bolt. *Daft old Ma'am.* His curiosity got the better of him. Raising his eyebrows, he looked at Rita, gave what he hoped was a nonchalant shrug and followed. Rita sighed and marched after him. The old lady was setting a brisk pace. Minutes later she stopped at Rita's houseboat.

It was bigger than it looked from a distance, with a little gangplank bridge from the path to the door, and a garden of potted impatiens and petunias. A cat crept over the roof and hid. Rita made encouraging noises. It jumped down and wound itself around her ankles.

She was about to unlock the door when a tall, amiable-looking man stepped out from behind the veranda.

"Oh Travis, I'm so sorry!"

His eyes flicked over Finn, but he nodded and smiled at May. His gaze returned to Rita. "Well, you're here now," he said. "That's the main thing." He chuckled. "You've obviously been on a jaunt."

Rita looked perturbed. "How long have you been waiting?

He looked at her with patent affection. "It's not a problem . . ." He looked as if he was about to add an endearment, but cleared his throat instead. "I've changed the reservation to 8:00." He paused, added lightly: "Er, did you forget your phone, then?"

"No. Well . . . yes." His face creased in puzzlement. "I'll explain later. I'm so sorry." She frowned at Finn and glanced accusingly at May, who was beaming. "We were kidnapped!"

"Kidnapped, is it!" I'll be looking forward to hearing about that."

"I'll meet you at the Three Swans, if that's OK. You go on ahead. There's something I . . . I . . . we . . ." she indicated her two companions . . . "we have to do first."

May continued to beam. Finn said nothing. He had the uncomfortable feeling he had seen this Travis before and the encounter had not been pleasant. *Where?* He bent nervously to play with the cat. It was now behind him on its hind legs, front paws peddling against the door. He turned round to stroke it. As he did so, he felt the back of his neck prickle in warning.

"Thief!" roared Travis. "You're nicked, you thieving little bastard! I'd know that hair-do anywhere!"

In a startled attempt to turn round again, Finn almost lost his balance.

May gave a little wail. Her face fell. "What!" said Rita, her voice deadly quiet. She turned to glare at

Finn, once more transformed into the fierce avenger of the swan encounter.

Travis took a step forward. "You tried to steal Jessie!"

Finn knew him at once. "You're that yelling farm hand." He stood his ground. "I only . . ."

"*Farm* hand?" Travis's voice sharpened with authority. "I'm in charge of the stables! I'm his lordship's head groom and trainer!"

May said gently: "Finn . . . ?"

"I wasn't *stealing* the horse." He drew himself up as straight as he could and said firmly: "I'm not a thief!"

"Oh, 'course not!" Travis scoffed. He looked him up and down, his eyes lingering again on Finn's hair. "The police said it was probably a gypo." He grimaced with distaste. He turned to Rita. "What the devil are you doing with . . .?" He turned to May with incomprehension on his face.

Calmly, with affronted dignity, Finn repeated: "I'm not a thief."

May chimed in. "But Finn . . . whatever were you . . . why?"

"I wanted a ride, just a ride. A trot, really. I was missing the fairs." He looked at Travis. "But when you started chasing me, I had to, well, I had to go a bit faster, didn't I? The devil got into me, I s'pose." He smiled at the recollection. "She's a sweet horse." He looked Travis full in the face. Ma had told him that the truth shines out through the eyes. He said simply: "I would've brought her back."

"I believe him," said May instantly.

Travis ignored her. His eyes narrowed. "Where, in god's name, did you learn to ride like that?"

Finn paused, a wry expression on his face. "Well," he shrugged, "I'm a *gypo*, aren't I."

Travis threw his hands up, turned on his heel and stomped over the gangplank to the towpath. Rita called after him: "See you later, OK?" Travis kept on walking. "Travis?"

"Yeah, yeah!"

"We'll . . . we'll talk about it."

He marched off down the path.

No one spoke.

Finn cleared his throat. "I think I'd better be going."

Still no one spoke. May was looking at Rita. Rita was staring after Travis.

"I told him the truth. Doesn't seem to matter much, does it?"

Rita looked at Finn, biting her lip. At last she met May's distressed gaze. Half a minute went by. Wordlessly, they appeared to have reached an uncomfortable agreement. Rita looked briefly at Finn and turned to unlock the door. She said briskly: "Well come in then." The cat shot in ahead of them.

Finn hung back. May looked round and held his gaze. His guard was down. He looked both offended and forlorn. She patted his arm. Then, trusting desperately that he would not walk away, she nodded towards Rita waiting for them inside and followed her. Finn hesitated. Once again, his curiosity prevailed. They followed Rita through a room of comfortable chaos, a door, a smaller room, a second door, and were instantly regaled with the pungent smell of paint. They were standing in a curved, airy space at the bow.

Finn, walking in behind them, stopped dead, open-mouthed. The room was a studio. It was full of tubes of paint, bottles of organic, orange-scented solvent, paper towels, rags, chutney jars bulging with assorted brushes. There were two easels. Empty canvases were stacked three-deep against the walls. One was enormous. A paint-spattered overall hung on a peg. Completed canvases hung everywhere, mostly of arresting landscapes. There were also some pictures of working dogs, and a few intriguing abstracts. They varied from highly competent to outstanding. There was a skylight and a big, floor-to-ceiling, sliding picture window down one side to catch the best of the light. The studio looked as if it had been left moments before. But if Finn had known it, it was a museum.

Rita had left it exactly as he had left it, her husband. He had gone off one winter's evening, whistling, to meet some friends at the pub. She was to join them after her shift at the veterinary practice. It was to be a celebration of their first year away from the rat race. But her husband had never arrived. A drunken group of joyriders had hit him as he was crossing the road. He had died at the scene.

Robert had been an enthusiastic artist and managed to sell a number of his paintings. He found an agent and sold more. On that basis they had left a more prosperous life in the city to find some fulfilment in doing what they liked and keeping to their own timetable. Robert had given up the law to follow his dream. Rita left a position in middle management to work with domestic animals. She was astonishingly attuned to them and was particularly good with the frightened ones. She also worked, via the veterinary practice, with an animal charity to find homes for the wretched strays sent over by the police or brought in by concerned members of the public. May had brought her several.

Robert and Rita had sold their town house with its study and hopeful nursery, and bought the big, comfortable houseboat outright. It was a serene existence. Until tragedy rendered it meaningless.

"Take whatever you need." Rita's voice was curter than she had intended. She was staring at an unfinished landscape on one of the easels. Her voice dropped to a whisper. "He would have approved."

Finn caught May's eye. She mouthed "husband," and pointed to her wedding finger, then mouthed "died." He looked puzzled. May closed her eyes and let her head fall back. He nodded. He walked slowly up to the easel and stood next to Rita. She was gazing at the picture, dry-eyed. He had the feeling she had no tears left.

"I . . ." He struggled. "I wouldn't know what to do with all this. I don't know *how* to . . . not like this . . ." He gestured round the room.

"Yes you do," said May sharply. "The gift. It isn't in your head. It's in your hands, in your heart."

"But what could *I* . . . ?" He turned to Rita. "Why . . . ?"

"Oh just . . . just *take* . . . !" She broke off and walked, unseeing, to the window. He saw she was lost, in a place where she could not find her way. He knew how that felt.

"Miss, er . . . um . . ." He went over to her. "I can't just . . ."

She turned to him, her eyes snapping: "Yes you can. You're as good as May says, that's obvious. Robert wouldn't want all this to go to waste. I've been saving it." Her voice tailed off. "Don't know what for." She stared at the floor. "You might as well."

"Wait a minute." May looked thoughtful. She approached Rita, put her arm around her and walked her to the other side of the room. Finn heard a hushed conversation. Rita frowned and looked over at him. May shook her head and began to talk earnestly. They looked at one another.

"Well?" whispered May. Rita bit her lip.

Finn was confused. "Look, I don't like to . . . it's OK, I don't need to . . . take . . . anything." His tone suggested he was still jangling at the word "thief".

May studied Rita's face, waiting. Slowly, Rita managed the ghost of a smile. May patted her arm and turned to him.

"You don't need to, no," she said. "We've had a better idea. Don't *take* anything! Work *here*. Paint, *here.* Long as you want, often as you want."

He was stunned. There was a fraught silence. "I have to babysit for my sister and all. I mean, it's getting late . . . they aren't really interested in . . . my brother-in-law won't . . . I can't just . . ." He could hear himself babbling.

"Whenever you can," May added kindly.

He looked at Rita for confirmation. She nodded. "I'll give you a key . . ." Looking distraught, Finn threw up his hands up in a stop-right-there gesture. "People see me coming in here, I'll be locked up fast as you can say gypo!"

May winced. Rita scarcely paused, went on as if he hadn't spoken. "I'll give you . . . *a Key.*" She looked full at him, her mouth set, ". . . *to the Big. Studio. Window.*" She ignored the protest he was about to make and ploughed on like a strict landlady. "The door into the rest of the houseboat will be locked. The front door will be locked . . ." She managed a gentler expression, taking pity on his discomfort. "But you can come and go through the sliding window whenever you want."

He said nothing.

She reverted to the brisk, no-nonsense voice, "I'll make sure everyone around here knows you have my permission."

"Yes," said May. "Now that your wonderful horse is on YouTube, we need a follow-up. We need . . ." She groped for the right words.

He paled, stared at the floor. His knuckles clenched, turned white. He was chewing the inside of his cheek.

". . . what we need is a bit of fanfare, eh, Finn?"

"May," cautioned Rita.

He looked up, his face a mask. "You want me to . . . to *produce* something . . . perform to order? Get involved in . . . pander to that . . . that . . . stupid circus?" He was not just distressed now, he was angry. "I can't do this! What am I . . ." he was shouting now, "an organ grinder's monkey?"

There was a stunned silence. No one moved.

Both women saw he was fighting for control of his temper and, more importantly, his dignity, which had already been tried in the encounter with Travis. He regarded May and managed a stiff little inclination of the head. "I'm grateful to you . . . May . . . er, ma'am . . ." He flinched at the distress on her face but kept to his resolve. "I . . . I . . ." He finished abruptly: "Thank you for the tea." He turned to Rita. "It was a . . . a fine offer, miss, so it was. I do thank you . . ." He paused fractionally, then added in a harsh, deathly quiet voice: "I'm done!"

He marched out.

There was a strained silence. They watched his retreating back as he swept past a mother with three small children who were squealing and chasing each other down the towpath. May said with conviction: "He'll come round, a talent like that, I know it." She faltered. Her voice wobbled. "He won't . . . he *can't* . . . let a chance like this go to waste."

"Oh May." Rita bit her lip. "I told you it wouldn't work. I told you. He's just a kid. What did we expect with the background he's had?"

May's face crumpled. "I shouldn't have pushed him."

Rita softened at once. "Right now, he's overwhelmed. Let him cool off. Let's just wait and see, eh?"

*   *   *

That evening, sitting opposite a still-irate Travis in the conservatory restaurant, Rita found to her surprise that she was defending Finn with a loyalty as fierce as her earlier antagonism. She told herself, with wry amusement, that she hadn't just been persuaded by May. She had somehow become a convert in her own right. She attempted to explain Finn's gift.

Travis wasn't buying it. He put his glass of Guinness down a little too hard, leaned forward and told her, in staccato sentences how the cheeky little bugger had sidled up to the mare and appeared to be having a chat with her. "Then he leapt on her back as if he thought he was in a bloody western."

Rita felt herself unexpectedly suppressing a smile. She managed with an effort to frown in sympathy.

Travis was at full throttle. "Saw it happen from the tack room window. Ran out and chased 'im. The kid saw me. Put Jessie to the gallop. Flat out."

"No saddle?"

"No saddle, no bridle, no nothing."

"Well he said all he wanted was a trot. I suppose he didn't mind where she went." Travis said nothing. She added carefully: "He does seem to have a way with horses."

"Probably because he's pinched so many!"

"No!" Her voice rose. The waitress, who had been hovering to take their order, retreated to a discreet distance. Rita hastily lowered her voice. "He's . . . Finn's not . . . He seems a serious boy."

"Well he wasn't serious tearing across that damn field! The trouble I had catching that horse, having to explain . . ."

"Travis," she said in earnest. "Have you . . . have you reported him? Have you been back to the police, I mean?"

He lifted his glass and drank, studying her over the glass. He put it down, stared at the table. There was a pause. "Not yet."

She patted his hand. He looked at her, saw her expression soften. He slapped the table in frustration. The waitress retreated again. "You've been brainwashed. Don't you know that? May's gone silly in her old age."

Rita gritted her teeth. She took out her phone. "Look at this! Finn's painting has had thousands of hits!"

He glanced at it and scoffed. "Belongs exactly where it is, is my view."

She took back the phone. "This is too small to get a proper look. Why don't you come and see the real painting, if it's still on the wall? We could go tomorrow." She patted his hand. "Oh come on! In the name of horses everywhere!"

Travis sighed. He sensed imminent defeat. Though . . . not, perhaps, a rout. He looked into her eyes and suppressed what threatened to be a sly smile.

"We . . . ell." He appeared to be wavering. "On one condition."

She tensed, studied him anxiously.

"Come with me to the Midsummer Ball."

"This is blackmail!" She tried to sound outraged. *He never gives up!* But she found, to her surprise, that she didn't mind too much.

The waitress visibly relaxed and approached the couple for the third time.

*   *   *

Finn was restless. On the building site with his brother-in-law, he was caught staring into space and ribbed for turning into a slacker. At home he played with Connor, but his sister noticed he was edgy and distracted.

"Wassup, me darlin'?" She put an arm around him.

"Kath, do you think . . .?" He stopped. She waited, but he refused to say any more.

A week went by. He made up his mind to go down and see May. He told himself he couldn't leave it like that. He owed her a proper apology. A posh bunch of flowers? He rejected the idea almost immediately.

Cheap shot. May's good opinion couldn't be bought. So he would just say his piece and be done with it. He hurried down the towpath and stopped in shock. The barge was no longer there.

*   *   *

He couldn't understand why he was so confused. He felt like an abandoned dog. He smiled slightly as he recalled Rita's first description of him, followed by May's triumphant "Wooof!" *Well, no help for it. Bite the bullet.* He marched down to Rita's houseboat and knocked. She wasn't there. *Might've known.* Then he wondered if she *was* there but just didn't want to open the door. *Gotta be thick skinned. Come on, pikey.* He went back twice more before he found her at home.

The door opened. "Finn!"

A succession of emotions flickered across her face. *Sun and clouds on a windy day.* He detected hope, defeat, trepidation and, albeit briefly, perhaps relief.

"I'm sorry to . . ." He faltered, abandoned courtesy. "Where's May?"

"I don't know, Finn."

"This is my fault. I've upset her."

"That's going a bit far. She was . . . disappointed. But she'll live."

"Is she coming back?"

"Next week, next year, you never know with May." Rita was pleasant, but reserved.

"I thought you were friends?"

"We are, but she often flits off somewhere. I wouldn't worry too much." She added more kindly: "Can I give her a message? She'll phone."

"N . . . I just wanted to . . ." His voice tailed off. He stared at the brightly painted boards under his feet. There was an awkward pause. He looked about absently for the cat.

"If you're worrying about Travis, you don't need to."

He looked at her sharply. "I didn't come here for . . ."

"He's decided to let the whole incident drop."

He stared, knew at once that this was her doing. His distraught expression relaxed, became warmer. "Thank you," he said simply. Rita heard the dignified gratitude in his voice.

Another pause. He obviously wanted to say something further, but she saw he was at a loss. He turned to go, went a few steps, hesitated, looked back.

She had quietly closed the door.

*   *   *

May deliberately did not tell Rita where she was going, though she thought she might guess. The old lady was more dismayed than she was willing to admit to her friend. She needed a change of scene. She had the ideal place in mind: the milling, constantly-changing array of narrow boats and enthusiastic bargers making new friendships, and unexpectedly renewing old ones, that epitomised Foxton Locks. There would be bargers she knew. It was inevitable. It was good to catch up, exchange gossip. And deep down, she wanted to talk about Finn to someone uninvolved. He had been, if only for a short while, her protégé.

It was a glorious day. She could smell the Queen Anne's Lace in the air, the gilly flowers and pansies nodding in rows down the series of locks, and the faint aroma of sheep in the rolling Leicestershire fields nearby. She strolled up and down the staircase of locks. It was dizzyingly steep. It never ceased to fill her with wonder at human ingenuity. She waved, shouted greetings, and watched the walkers and tourists. The walkers were usually old hands. They would stand for a while, chat to the lock keeper, then hike on, or duck into the Inn for refreshments and a snack.

She found the tourists more entertaining. They were usually either in twos or in families. Always a mix of nationalities. She could predict their squeals of delight as they witnessed the emptying and filling of a lock for the first time. They would join in the camaraderie of the place, shouting greetings to complete strangers and exchanging banter. Some pointed out how the locks worked to wide-eyed children or lent a hand when the machinery proved too tricky for somebody to manipulate alone.

To May, it felt like home. She had been born near here and had loved barges all her life, watching them come and go, wondering about the lives of the people she would glimpse for a few minutes before they disappeared, briefly touching her life. She had vowed that one day she would have a canal boat of her own. And here she was.

A couple of hours later she found herself having lunch at the Inn with a cheery group of bargers. She'd met Al and Trish from Liverpool and their dog, Norman, (of bewildering parentage) two years ago on the waterways of France. The American couple, Bonny and Asa from Orange County, New York, were new friends. They were open-minded and sociable in the disarmingly American tradition. They had brought along their teenage son, Howard, and daughter, Bryony, who did not seem at all bored by their parents, or their parents' friends. May was astonished. They found the whole narrow boat thing "kinda cool" and were busy texting their friends and sending pictures. The youngest daughter, Sophie, was a different matter. She was on a permanent rant to her friends back home. Her default reaction to being addressed was to roll her eyes and mutter: "Jeez, this sucks."

"So May, where's Duffie?"

"Gone fishin'!

Everybody laughed.

"No, really. He's up with some cronies in Scotland crashing through mountain streams and telling tall tales."

"By a camp fire?"

"Hah!" Her voice rose incredulously. "Roughing it at their age? No!" She laughed. "They're up at a five-star hotel! Moving to a B&B further up the glen next week. Apparently, there's a brilliant pub next door."

"That's what it's all about," said Al and raised his glass to May.

"He'll be down here in September, before we go home for the winter."

Everyone except Sophie was smiling. They ate for a few minutes in companionable silence.

Al bent down. "Want a crisp Norman? *Crisp?* The dog lifted his lip in a snarl and, confusingly, wagged his tail. Even Sophie, watching him covertly, giggled. He demolished a handful of crisps. Playing to his audience, he lifted a paw for somebody to shake hands. May obliged. He wagged his tail again and growled.

"Weird, isn't it?" said Trish. "Come on, Norman, give us a kiss." She leaned down. The dog turned bashful, rolling his eyes and hanging his head like a nervous schoolboy. "Norman, kisses!" Without warning, the dog threw himself at Trish and enthusiastically licked her ear. She turned to the amused spectators. "Oh give him his applause or there'll be no living with him." They laughed aloud and clapped. Norman collected further perks as more crisps appeared in hands under the table.

There was a comfortable silence.

"So, what's new, May?" It was Al.

"We . . . ll . . ." said May. She hesitated. They all looked at her expectantly. She cleared her throat. "You won't believe this, but . . . well . . . there were these young thugs and a swan and . . ." They leaned forward, elbows on the table. She proceeded to tell them about Finn. They listened, fascinated. Sophie pretended she wasn't interested.

"Wow," said Howard. "A real gypsy, How cool is that?"

"I think he'd prefer "traveller", said May.

Bryony chimed in. I think "gypsy" is more romantic."

Their mother was more thoughtful. "You know, May, I think you shouldn't give up on him. He's just a dumb ass kid. He can't see the canal for the boats."

It wasn't the profound insight she had been looking for, but it made her smile.

"You know what I think?" said Al. "That lad needs a good, swift boot up the backside." May pictured somebody attempting to do this to Finn and burst out laughing.

Her amusement ceased abruptly. Her hand flew to her mouth. Everyone looked round. He was standing facing her a few feet from the table.

There was an uncomfortable pause. *Oh god. How much has he heard?*

"Hello, Finn."

His expression was wary. But she saw beneath it, resolve. He was staring at her, about to say something, when Bryony burst out: "Hey, is that him?"

Finn stared at her, white-faced. He looked round the circle of faces. His eyes narrowed when they settled on Al. May knew at once that he must have heard. He looked at her again. His guard was up and he was bristling.

"Come on, kid, sit down and have a bite to eat! World's not gonna end!" It was Asa. "And stop glaring, for Christ's sake. We're all friends here!"

The man's unexpected bluffness and good humour de-fused some of Finn's antagonism. He had not encountered such forthrightness before outside the family.

"May's told us a lot of great things about you," Asa went on. "Come on, sit down." He nodded at an unused chair at the next table.

Finn didn't move. *Be arsed if I will.* But his feathers were noticeably less ruffled.

Sophie came to life. "You don't look much like a gypsy to me! Don't you wear earrings?" She leaned forward coyly. "Will you tell my fortune?"

"Sophie!" It was her mother.

May was further mortified. But once more in their brief acquaintance, Finn surprised her. He turned to the American girl. "I can't tell your fortune, girly, but I can see you're going to break a lot of hearts." The girl flushed with pleasure.

But he was not to be diverted. He turned to May. "Can I talk to you? Please?" He had deliberately not lowered his voice. He despised that kind of furtiveness. It seemed underhand.

It was May's turn to be defensive, although she kept her voice level. She didn't want to sound too hopeful. "You can talk to me here, Finn. I don't think we have anything private to discuss, do we?"

He flinched. May saw his chin come up.

Asa gave him a jovial thump on the back. "Like I said, all friends here."

Finn responded with a faint smile, came to an apparent conclusion, nodded to himself and turned to go.

May relented and called out: "All right." She stood up. "All right, Finn. Let's go and talk outside." She turned to her friends. "Carry on. We won't be long."

Outside, she could see how jangled he was. She studied him, frowning. He was staring into the distance.

"Never seen locks like this before. Quite a sight."

"How did you find me?"

He offered a faint smile. "Pestered Rita. She wasn't sure. But I thought it was worth a try."

"But Finn . . ." She paused. "Why?"

He gazed up at dabs of cloud floating over a periwinkle-blue sky. "Well I wanted to . . . er . . ." She waited. He looked down at his feet. Silence. "You um . . . don't have any of that special brew, do you . . . uh . . . *ma'am.*" He had intended to tack it on wryly. What May heard was a kind of agitated sadness. There was a tense pause. At last he looked at her. She smiled at him carefully. "Of course."

They walked in awkward silence to the barge. It was moored not far from the upper lock. She went at once to the kitchen.

"Ma'am . . ."

She turned to look at him. "Sit down, Finn. Please."

He hesitated. "I came to apologise. I was ungrateful and rude." He pressed on. He had clearly been rehearsing what he wanted to say. "You've given me such encouragement. Wouldn't have occurred to me on my own. You believed in me. Not many people have done that. Just wanted to tell you I appreciate it, that's all." He saw that she was somewhat gratified. He also saw the hurt beneath it and hated himself. "Oh, I . . . uh . . ." He thrust a bunch of wild flowers at her. He had picked them on the long walk through the fields. Touched, she saw that they had wilted inside his jacket. She took them, rose on tiptoe and pecked him on the cheek. "I only wanted the best for you, you know that." She squeezed his arm.

"Yeah. I know." His poise wavered. "Well, thanks anyway." He walked to the door.

"I thought you wanted some tea?"

"I . . . I think I'd better be off." He turned to go.

"Do you have a mobile number?"

"Wh . . . What? Nah. Declan does, for work."

Would you write it down for me?"

"Uh . . . sure."

She held out a biro and the back of an envelope. He scribbled the number and handed it to her. She could see he was oddly gratified.

"Must be on my way." He walked to the door.

"Er, Finn, before you go . . ." He turned his head. " . . . Can I ask you something?"

She detected a slight wariness in his expression, but he was listening.

"Have you ever painted anything else? I mean, besides the horse?"

He grinned at her. "The chicken coop, last week."

She sighed, raised her eyebrows and waited.

He looked away. His eye fell on a photograph on the wall. It was of a much younger May standing next to a youthful bride and groom. A robust and pleasant-looking man stood, bursting with pride, on their other side.

"Nah."

"Nothing?"

He was shaking his head when something struck him.

May's pulse quickened.

He cleared his throat self-consciously. "Well, er . . . Nah. Not really."

"Not really?"

"It wasn't painting. It . . ." he hesitated, then added with finality, "it was nothing." He was clearly not going to say anything else.

"Well tell me anyway," May wheedled with a smile. She could see he was debating with himself.

Silence.

She waited. The silence lengthened, became uncomfortable.

At last he sighed: "It's stupid."

She waited.

"I used to, well, sort of draw people. Whenever we went to the fairs.

"What . . . what did you draw them with?"

He looked at her as if she were crazy. "A pencil, what else?

"Did they sit for you?"

"Sit?"

"Pose, sit still?"

"Yeah, but not for long. I had to rush it or they'd be gone. It was nothing really. Just mucking about. They'd give me a couple of quid and I'd give it to Ma. She thought it was daft, but she was pleased with the cash. And she'd stop nagging at me for a bit. Same as when I won races. You know. The horses."

"Finn," said May carefully, "do you have any of those drawings?"

Don't be daft. "The people took them, didn't they. They probably had a good laugh and chucked 'em in the rubbish. But I had the last laugh, cos I got the money. Look, I should really be getting off home now . . ."

May leaned forward and said lightly: "Would you draw me?"

His expression suggested that she had just asked him if he'd like to go to Mars.

"For a fee, of course," she added.

He looked uncomfortable, perplexed. He ran a hand through his hair. "If . . . if you want." He added hurriedly: "I wouldn't expect you to pay anything, mind." His chin came up. "Ma's back in Galway and my sister wouldn't . . . wouldn't take it."

"I'll pay you a fee . . ." He raised his hands to refuse. ". . . A fee," she repeated. "And you'll just have to lump it!"

He made a face, then chuckled in genuine amusement. *Ma'am likes to get her way, so she does.*

"Didn't it ever occur to you to keep some of the money yourself, buy a few things?"

Silence. He was staring out of the window at a big family with a pushchair strolling along the towpath.

"What about now, with my fee?"

She saw his chin come up. He looked at her. "I help Declan. He works in construction, so I earn a bit. I play with Connor and take him out. They feed me and give me a bed. We're family." There was a barely discernible pause. "Don't need much."

"She took a risk. "But you're not that happy, are you?"

"Don't know what you mean."

"Yes you do."

He kicked his foot back and forth and stuffed his hands in his pockets.

She said hastily: "Are you going to draw me or not?"

He huffed, bit his lip. "When?"

"How about now?"

"Now? Won't your friends be waiting for you?"

"Hah! They'll be there for hours." She got up and went to the little mahogany bureau. "More people will drop in on them, go away again. Somebody will bring a guitar. We're all staying overnight. Nobody's in a rush.

She handed him an HB pencil, a large sheet of vellum and an eraser. He handed the eraser back as if she had insulted him. Her eyebrows went up, but she said nothing.

"How do you want me to pose?"

"Doesn't matter. However you want." He looked round, indicated a little occasional chair near the window.

She settled forward in the chair, the full glow of summer light on her face. "No need to rush, Finn, I haven't any urgent appointments."

"Yeah, well I've got to get home . . ."

"So get on with it, then." She cupped her chin in her hand and leaned on the sill.

He rolled his eyes at the ceiling. *Just like Ma.* He looked about, grabbed the tea tray and turned it over as a drawing board. Then he sat down on the arm of the sofa. At once, he was intent. He studied her for a full two minutes as if he were assessing her entire being. Then he set to work.

She watched the metamorphosis from nonchalance to an absorption that excluded all else. But she was puzzled. He scarcely looked at her. *Well, he said his subjects probably had a good laugh. Perhaps it'll be a cartoon.* She sat quietly and said nothing.

Twenty minutes later he put down his pencil and stood up. He made an ironic face. "That will be two pounds, ma'am." He handed her the picture and bowed. "Aye do hope you like it."

She stared at it and found, suddenly, that she could not breathe. An agitated bird began struggling to get out of her chest. She looked up at him. He was watching her with cool amusement. His intensity had dissipated like mist. He was a boy once more, with nothing but a bit of blarney on his face.

The silence lengthened.

"It's . . . er, not that bad, is it?"

"It's . . ." she managed, almost speechless. "This is . . . Finn, this is wonderful."

He laughed dismissively. "I'm no Picasso."

"No." She almost choked, tried to collect herself. "You're Thomas Lawrence! God in heaven, you are!"

"Never heard of him. Who's he, then, somebody local?"

He's . . . he was . . . just like you. Oh Finn, this is exquisite. So delicate, so subtly done. It's . . . I think you . . . I think you've caught my soul."

He turned scarlet, stuffed his hands in his pockets, took them out again. "I . . . I've gotta go." He ran a hand through his hair. "My sister . . .

May was incapable of further speech.

He managed a jaunty smile. But she could see it was drastically at odds with something else in his face, as if something dormant had suddenly woken and ignited. He gave her a determinedly casual wave and sauntered out.

She sat for a long while gazing at the picture, her hand to her mouth. Much later she realized she had not given him his fee.

*   *   *

Finn walked home across the bright fields in such a state of agitation that he was forced to stop and sit down. He sprawled under a gnarled old oak, staring up through the leaves until his heart was beating less wildly.

The next day, Kath found him sketching the baby. She peered over his shoulder. "That's nice, Finn. Why don't we send it to Ma for her birthday, eh?"

"Kath, do you think . . ." This time there was urgency in his voice. "I mean . . . ?" But he didn't know what it was he was trying to say.

"Do I think what? Come on, you've got to tell me now." She waited. "Some girl, I bet, yer handsome devil."

He shook his head, gave up and went out.

"Don't you be late for your dinner, now. It'll be an hour." She stared after his slowly retreating back. He stopped suddenly, as if something had occurred to him. She watched him take his hands out of his pockets and quicken his pace. *Now* where was he off to? He worried her.

He went straight to the library. He wanted to find out just who this Thomas Lawrence was. *Sir* Thomas Lawrence, he discovered. He gaped at the finesse of the drawings the man had tossed off from the age of ten (*Ten?*) and recognized with shock a self-taught talent that did, indeed, suggest his own. May was right. He studied the pictures with care, especially the ones with a touch of pastel: the palest rose in a cheek, the barely-there outline of a splendid hat.

Then he turned to the great procession of oil portraits, famous people most of them. He was thunderstruck. His hands trembled. No *training*? No *nothing*? And little Tommy Lawrence had ended up president of the Royal Academy? A pretty barongo achievement for the penniless son of an innkeeper. *Jesus, Mary and Joseph!*

*   *   *

On Tuesday, after carting bricks and mixing mortar with Declan, he headed for Rita's houseboat. This time there was resolution and purpose in his stride. He knocked. There was no answer. He called out. "It's Finn! I came to tell you." He knocked again. "Changed my mind." He heard someone moving about inside. "I'd really like to have a go. In a proper studio, like you said."

The door flew open. He flinched at her expression and stepped back. "Old, doesn't see too well, especially when there isn't much light. Poor May! Nice of you to string her along!" She advanced, her expression fierce. "Not to mention me." "You *had* to walk out, didn't you?" In spite of himself, he backed again. "You and your "I can't do this!" All that phoney outrage!" She took an aggressive step towards him. "And you *couldn't* do it, could you? We called your bluff and the game was up."

Finn paled. He said nothing.

She jabbed at him with her finger. "The wonder horse by the canal was painted by a twenty-two year old art student. He did it for a dare. His name is Porter Gordon Spears. Pogy, for short. It's been all over YouTube since last night." Her voice rose to a shout. "Go *away*!" She attempted to slam the door in his face. He grabbed, barely managed at the last moment to hold it back and narrowly missed having his fingers crushed.

"I'm the perfect pikey, aren't I!" He forced the door open. "First I'm a thief . . ." He almost spat it out. He glared at her. "First word you ever said to me was "Scum!" His voice rose to a yell. "Well what did you expect from a *gypo*?"

There was a fraught silence.

"So you're telling me you *did* paint the horse?" Her tone was low and bitterly sarcastic.

He said nothing.

She yelled back: "This Pogy Spears is the liar, then, is he?"

He flung up his arm in a dismissive gesture. "The hell with it!" Shoulders squared, hands balled into fists, he banged across the gangplank and marched off. "Think what you bloody well like!"

*   *   *

May came back the next morning in a state of barely contained excitement. "Rita, you'll never guess . . ." She was brought up short by her friend's expression.

"Did he find you?"

"Yes. Yes, he did." Her jubilation was bubbling over. "You've got to see this. It's . . ." She stopped again. "What . . . what is it?"

Rita told her.

May's eyes widened in shock. She said at once: "Twaddle! The boy's a publicity seeker, cashing in because nobody else came forward!"

"May," Rita was exasperated. "It can't have been . . ." She corrected herself hastily, ". . . might not have been Finn you saw. It was at night . . ."

"A bright, moonlit night, as I recall. Don't patronize me, Rita. It was Finn."

Rita refused to be put off. She said gently: "You know you won't wear your glasses." May bridled. "Duffie told me. He said it was your only vanity." May said nothing. Attempting to de-fuse the situation with an awkward touch of humour, Rita added: "Remember that night we were on our way to the poetry reading and you jumped out of your skin because you thought a parking meter had just moved, when it was Mr Harris?"

"Well he shouldn't have been lurking. Standing there like a lump, rooted to the spot!" Anyone could have . . ."

Rita's voice rose in consternation. "Look at this, May." She produced her phone, fiddled and held it up for her to see. "This young man. He's older, but he does look a bit like Finn. You know you saw him mostly from behind, when he was painting. And they've both got long hair."

May stared at the photo. Rita could not read her expression. She pressed her advantage. "This young man is trained, experienced . . ."

"This young man is a liar!" May sat down abruptly in the kitchen chair where Rita had been enjoying the luxury of a late breakfast. She hadn't slept well.

Rita ploughed on. "We've only Finn's word for it. Well, not even that. He came to see me yesterday. We had a confrontation."

"Oh Rita!" She searched her friend's face. "Didn't he deny it?"

"No. Well . . . sort of. Well . . . not exactly." Silence. "You could take what he said either way." She rushed on. "I told him to get lost. He stomped off in a rage."

"Poor Finn."

"Think about it. Think. Remember how agitated he was when you took us on the barge to see the horse. You were making him feel so important. He must have felt guilty as hell. But don't you see? He just couldn't resist playing along."

The silence lengthened into a minute, two. She studied May's face anxiously. It was a distressing task to disillusion such a well-meaning and trusting friend. May was staring, unseeing, at a jug of orange juice.

Rita's discomfort increased, then turned to bewilderment, as she watched May's expression shift slowly from dismay to a sad smile and then suddenly assert itself in a rush of excitement that brought her to her feet.

"Let's suppose you're right, Rita. Suppose *all* of you are right." She nodded at the phone still in her friend's hand. "Suppose I did make a mistake. Even if I did, and even if he's human enough to have enjoyed the attention, and just wanted some wholehearted approval for a change . . ." she put her hand on Rita's arm, ". . . it doesn't matter a pin. Doesn't matter. Because . . . she opened the blue folder she was still holding, "he certainly *did* do this!" And *this*," she held up Finn's drawing, "is astonishing."

Rita didn't look at the picture. She continued to stare, exasperated, at her friend. "I don't care what he did, May. You remember what he said when he turned down my offer and walked out of the studio? She growled in mimicry: "I'm done!" Well this has gone on long enough. *I'm* done, too." She glanced at the drawing, too jangled to take in more than meaningless lines.

"Rita, he doesn't understand what he has. He doesn't realize. Look! Look at it!"

Determined to make May see sense, Rita barrelled on: "I'm sorry May, but he couldn't possibly be . . ." And then the lines in front of her suddenly coalesced into a masterly portrait. She broke off, incredulous.

"Yes, that was my reaction as well."

In the stunned silence that followed, May propped the drawing on the counter top between a salt pig and a bottle of olive oil. They continued to stare at it. The portrait compelled like a magnet. Rita felt as if she had gone down too quickly in a lift.

"He didn't even need an eraser."

"You're *sure* he did this? Could someone else have . . .?"

"Rita!" May burst out in a flare of unaccustomed impatience. "For goodness sake! *I* suggested it on the spur of the moment. He was drawing *me*. I was there. Don't be silly."

Rattled, they looked at one another. Little sparks of energy seemed to be rippling through the kitchen. Rita looked back at the portrait, scarcely able to think.

May could restrain herself no longer. "Whatever the truth is, can't we give him the benefit of the doubt?" She nodded at the portrait. "You're as astonished as I was. So what do we have to lose, really? Oh Rita, let him have a chance to mess about with paint, see what he can do, and without any pressure." She touched her friend lightly on the arm. "Why not?"

*   *   *

Next day, although Rita was still prickly, she knew enough about art to recognize the drawing's precocious skill and quality and had enough sense of fairness to acknowledge it. During her lunch break at the surgery, egged on by May, who had dropped by for that very purpose, Rita put her reservations aside and wrote Finn a note.

She would not apologise, she said. But she had reconsidered, after seeing May's drawing. She admitted he had "considerable promise", that it would be a pity to waste it, and she would give him free run of the studio as per her previous offer, if he was still interested. She would not . . .

At this point they were interrupted by a burst of barking from the waiting room, where two, over-excited dogs were having an altercation. Rita stuck her head through the door. The owners were wrestling to keep their nervous pets apart. She shouted to the receptionist over the din. "Give them a Bonio each, Dana!" She came back and picked up her pen." The uproar stopped abruptly. "Doesn't always work, but . . . Now, where was I?"

She picked up her pen. She would not, she went on, enter the studio unless invited, whether or not he was there, and he could do whatever he pleased. He would be answerable to no one at all. He would not be pushed or cajoled . . . May smiled at this, imagining Finn's expression: *Cajoled?* . . . Rita went on to say that if he wanted to remain anonymous, she was cool with that. She finished by instructing him, somewhat off-handedly: "Just enjoy yourself, OK?"

Next morning Declan received a baffling call. He turned to Kath and Finn at the breakfast table. "Some woman wants to know where the construction site is. Sounds a bit posh. "Just the directions, please," she says. No name." He looked hard at Finn. "You know anything about this?" Finn wondered briefly, then stared miserably at his plate and shook his head. Declan noted Kath's face, creased with worry these days whenever she looked at Finn, and wondered, not for the first time, what was going on. All Kath had said was that she was worried about him. Well, best leave it to her. He sighed and sat down to finish his breakfast. "Come on, boyo, finish yer toast, we've got to get going."

When they knocked off for a tea break at around 10:30, Declan made his customary announcement: "Going to turn my bike round," and hurried off to the Portaloo.

May saw her chance. The other men on the site were too preoccupied with their tea to notice her. She thought ruefully how often, in the distant past, she would have attracted the instant attention of males on building sites. Every week, she and her friends used to tally up their quota of wolf whistles.

She needed to get Finn's attention, but he was sitting by himself, staring blankly at his boots. She decided that boldness was the best course, hissed and made agitated hand signals to the man sprawled nearest to her in a loud and chatty group. When he looked across she beckoned and mimed her lack of a hard hat. He strolled over, eyebrows raised enquiringly.

"Can I help you?"

Oh, yes, you certainly can, Mr . . . er ?"

"Frank."

"Yes, well, could you hand that boy over there a note from his sister? She wants him to do some errands for her before he comes home."

"Oh." He hesitated, curious, then nodded, faint annoyance on his weather-beaten face. "Right."

As he turned, May felt she had better disappear, at least temporarily.

"Yo, Finn, message for you." He waved the note. Finn looked up and came over. "What's up with you, boy? Face as long as a week in Birmingham!" The man gulped from his mug of tea and handed him the envelope. Finn took it warily. "Ta." The man nodded and re-joined his pals.

He wondered if he was in trouble, but the envelope didn't look official. He opened it and began to read. She saw him drop the envelope in shock. He looked around, searching. She gave him a little wave from behind a 'Health and Safety Warning' sign. She beckoned. He looked behind him, probably checking to see where Declan was. She had a quick look herself. He had evidently turned his bike round and was chatting to a mate. He had his back to her. Finn sidled over and joined her behind the sign.

"I'm just the messenger."

He was biting his lip, clearly in a quandary.

She rushed on in case he decided to stomp off again. "Rita can be stubborn, but she wouldn't have sent you this unless she meant it."

"She's told you all about . . . ?"

"Yes, yes, never mind about that now." She indicated the letter he was holding. "All you have to do is say "yes". Oh, and look in the envelope. It's over there. You dropped it."

He paused, staring at her. Then he went over to the torn envelope and picked it up. He looked inside and raised his shoulders, puzzled.

She mimed he should look about on the ground. Still not knowing what he was looking for, he bent down. Moments later he held up his find. She nodded and smiled. It was the studio key.

*   *   *

When Rita had first told Travis that Finn was a fraud, he went ballistic. It had been hard to convince him not to go belatedly to the police. He was incredulous. "You're mad as hellfire, and still you're defending him?"

"All he stole from *you* was a ride. Let's not . . . let's not stoop to spite."

It was even trickier to bring Travis round to the idea that Finn was getting another chance in the studio. He rolled his eyes and looked mulish until Rita asked May to show him the portrait. He studied it, shaking his head. "OK, yes. Pretty good." He couldn't resist adding: "But you'll be sorry."

Kath and Declan agreed they could spare Finn for most of Saturday, though he hadn't said what for. But they needed him to watch Connor on Saturday night. They weren't sure yet about Sunday.

If Kath was puzzled, she was also relieved. Whatever had been troubling Finn was gone. Or rather, his restlessness had turned into a barely contained excitement.

The next day she found out why.

She and Declan stared at him open-mouthed. "You want to what?"

"I wasn't going to tell you yet . . . Just wanted to see if . . . if I could do it first."

"Do what? I mean, *paint?* . . . paint *what* exactly?" It was Declan.

Finn gave him an enigmatic smile. It broadened as he recognized his brother-in-law's confusion. "Don't know yet." "I'll still be helping you at the site, Dec. I always do the job, you know that. Won't let you down. Or you, Sis." He put his arm around her. "No need to worry about Connor." Her frown disappeared instantly, like lines in a wrinkle cream ad.

Declan blew out his breath. "We . . . ll . . ." His bluff, impish face was solemn. "All right, then." He attempted to smile. "Tell us in your own good time, eh, boyo? Sure you must think you know what you're doing." He slapped Finn on the back and ruffled his hair. "You *do* know you're probably crazy, kid?"

"Yeah," said Finn, and grinned.

*   *   *

He stood in the middle of the studio, overwhelmed. Rita had removed all Robert's paintings, clearly wanting it to be ready when he changed his mind. He bit his lip. She had known him better than he knew himself. He looked round with rising excitement. She had left everything else, including all the blank canvases. He felt thoroughly humbled.

First thing to do? He looked about, bewildered by choice. *Right. Put on the overall.* It was still there on its peg. He took it off again at once. *Can't be him. Shouldn't. 'S not right.* He poked about, found an old sheet in a corner and wrapped it around him. *Better.*

It hampered him as he clambered onto a high stool at the draughting table. He grinned. He probably looked like Frodo in the spider's lair. He was sure he looked like an idiot. Or as Kath would say, "an eejet".

His excitement heightened as he examined the tubes of oils with proprietary delight. He looked around, grabbed a disposable palette and a broken knife handle and began to experiment with mixing colours. It was harder than it looked. It took him two days before he could create the exact shades and hues he visualised. He smeared them about with his fingers, got the feel of it. At last he was satisfied.

He turned to the bewildering array of brushes. *Jesus!*

*   *   *

Rita had kept Robert's paintings she liked best, including the unfinished landscape. She hung that in her bedroom. She had also contacted Robert's former agent, Henry Pierce, to tell him that she was, at last, ready to sell the remainder. Delighted, he agreed to stop by when he got back from Italy. He was leaving next morning.

Finn came and went without fuss. At first they were too uncomfortable to do more than nod to each other. Rita occasionally stopped by with a drink and a sandwich, but she always knocked. He never asked her in. He was usually utterly absorbed and rarely said anything except to mutter a distracted "thank you." Sometimes he didn't answer her knock at all. She would put the tray down outside the door and leave him to it.

Three weeks later Travis happened to mention to Rita that a commission for a horse painting might be coming up soon. "Pity the kid's a fraud. He loves his horses, I'll grant you that. Not the same thing as painting them though, is it!"

Next day, when Finn came to the door with splotches of different coloured paints up his right arm and across his forehead, Rita remarked that up at The Hall they were discussing having a portrait done of their best horse, Flying Dutchman. "It's for the sitting room, apparently." Rita was pursuing this only for

May. She strove to keep her face neutral. "Are you . . . are you interested?"

"You know I can't paint horses!" he shot back.

Rita sighed. "I don't know if you can or if you can't, but I thought you might like to give it a go."

"Just in case?"

She looked him in the eye. "Just in case."

"Well I wouldn't want to string you along."

Rita pursed her lips and glared. "Yes or no?"

Infuriatingly, he replied: "Tell you tomorrow," and closed the door.

Next day he left an appallingly drawn horse taped to the studio door. Underneath was a scribbled note. "Will this do?"

Rita tried to feel insulted, but laughed instead. The acrimony between them was dissolving into relentless banter. With relief she realized the hatchet was buried.

The next time he was in the studio she tried again. When he came to the door, she raised an eyebrow and said in a more conversational tone: "So are you going to have a go at Flying Dutchman?"

Finn paused, fiddled with the brush he was still holding. "They won't want me. I'm nobody. Nobody at all."

There was an awkward pause. "Why not do it just for fun?" Her tone was carefully light. "And then, if you're happy with it, and it's . . . er . . . well, accept . . ."

"Not too embarrassing?"

"Not too embarrassing," she continued, deadpan, "Travis can show it to them at least." She forestalled what she thought he was about to say with: "They haven't got around to commissioning anybody yet."

Maybe they'll ask Pogy Spears."

*   *   *

Travis was happily aware that he was making headway with Rita. The last thing he wanted was to rock the boat. Hence, a few days later, albeit reluctantly and still off-hand, he arranged for Finn to visit the stables "properly and above board." His face had been stern and unrelenting. Rita drove Finn over.

They crossed the stable yard, heading for Flying Dutchman's box. When the horse saw Travis, the chestnut pricked its ears and nickered softly. Then it saw Finn behind him. Tossing its head it nickered again. As Finn reached up to stroke it, the horse nuzzled his ear.

"I'll be damned!" said Travis under his breath.

"Told you," said Rita.

"Weird," agreed the stable boy, leaning on a fork. 'E only does that if 'e knows you." He looked at Finn suspiciously, trying to think if he'd seen him before.

The horse, whose yard name was Eric, nickered a second time and nuzzled Finn's hair.

"I'll be damned!" said Travis again.

Finn turned to him. "Can I . . .?"

"No! Just look! All right?"

Finn treated him to a wry grin. "I was going to say: "Can I watch him exercise? Need to see how he moves."

Travis scowled.

*   *   *

May had flitted off again.

"Haven't seen her for days, said Finn, as he stood in the studio doorway. "Boat's still there, though."

"She's up in Derbyshire at a ruby wedding bash," said Rita, handing him a mug of hot chocolate. "Careful, it's hot." She was sorely tempted to snatch a quick look past him into the studio, but restrained herself firmly by shifting position. "Former neighbours, apparently." He nodded and sipped. "They've invited her to stay on a bit afterwards. She'll be back soon."

When May eventually did come back, she went straight down to the houseboat.

"How's he getting on?"

Rita smiled. "I expect you want to see him?" May nodded. "He's here now. But I'd better warn you. Sometimes he doesn't open the door." She saw the question on May's lips: "Don't ask me what he's painting. He won't let me see." She added archly: "And I don't ask."

She paused. "He did sit and sketch me once on the veranda when I was watering the plants. But he must have changed his mind." She shrugged at May. "After about ten minutes he just got up and left." May cocked her head at that, wondering.

They made their way to the studio.

It was Rita who knocked. No answer. She waited. "Finn?" She knocked again. "May's back. She's come to see you."

There was a muffled crash. They heard scuffling noises, muttering. "Sounds as if he's trying to tidy up," whispered May. Rita nodded. They waited. At last he opened the door. He stood in his paint-spattered sheet like an ancient Roman in a toga.

"I'll leave you to it," said Rita. She moved back.

He looked flustered. But he was grinning. He bowed. "Do come in, ma'am." He stood back for her to enter. She noted a number of canvases that had been turned the wrong way round and nodded in their direction.

"I see you've been busy."

He hesitated. "Just been experimenting, mostly."

"Mostly?"

He pretended not to understand. "Never used oils before."

May threw caution to the winds. "Are you going to let me . . . ?"

"No!" He paused. "Not yet." He looked at her earnestly. "Your opinion matters to me. I don't want to let you down, either of you." He motioned for her to sit. He had cleared a small stool and, touchingly, had covered it with his jacket. "I'm working on . . . a few things . . . and something special." He indicated a very large canvas facing the wall. "I think you might like it. But it's taking a dog's age."

She nodded, tried not to look disappointed, knew she would have to be content with that. She managed a smile. "How are your family taking it? Do they know about . . ." She flung her arms wide and gestured to take in the whole studio . . . "all this?"

He chuckled. "I've squared it with them, both of them. They're OK with it. Just don't really understand. They think I'm crazy.

*   *   *

Travis was sworn to secrecy. "Well?" said Rita. "He wants to remain anonymous. Will you do as he asks?"

"I don't see the poin . . ."

May cut him off. "Finn doesn't want to have to . . . to deal with people . . . Not yet."

"I'll bet he doesn't!"

"Too much for him," she added firmly. She raised her voice and looked at him pointedly. "I'm sure we can all understand that?"

Travis huffed and looked at Rita, who had raised her eyebrows expectantly. He made a face and stared at the ceiling. Then he nodded abruptly. "All right, all right. You win. Can't fight both of you." His expression made it clear he thought the whole idea was a load of hogwash. He tapped the side of his nose ironically. "Mum's the word."

Rita nodded with satisfaction. But May insisted: "You haven't sworn yet.

Obligingly, he burst out: "When exactly are we going to see this fucking horse?" He scowled at both of them. "There! Will that do?"

May's lips twitched

"He said you can pick it up today around 5:00," said Rita. She glanced at her watch and smiled up at him.

*   *   *

They saw the painting ahead of them as they approached the studio. It stood on a stool outside the door, propped against the wall. All three came to an abrupt halt.

May's face crumpled. She uttered a plaintive little cry, her arm floundering behind her for a chair. She sank into it, swayed and covered her face with her hands. Tears began to trickle through her fingers. Rita studied the floor in silence, her hand on May's shoulder.

Travis rubbed the back of his neck and stared at it. He kept his mouth firmly clamped. He was saying nothing.

The studio door opened. Finn peered out enquiringly, his expression unreadable. "Will that do?"

As Rita met his eye she detected faint amusement. She said evenly: "If you could pack it, Travis will take it over tonight."

*   *   *

Up at the Hall they had a shock. Travis stood next to the picture, steadying it on an antique table and gauging their reaction. Lord and Lady H were confused.

"What on earth . . . ?" It was Lord H. "That's . . . How the devil . . . ?" He felt the need to sit down. "Good lord!"

"Seems that a painter friend . . ." Travis began, ". . . of a friend of mine (which was, after all, true) was so taken with the horse when he saw him at exercise that he er, painted him, milord."

"Just like that?"

"Just like that. Loves horses, it seems.

Lord H took his glasses off, put them on again and peered at the painting in silence. It was Flying Dutchman to the life, coat gleaming, neck extended, joyous, at full gallop and without a rider. The horse epitomised freedom. It was also an exquisite and masterly study in the fluidity of movement.

Travis went on: "It occurred to me, milord, that . . . well . . . perhaps you might be interested, seeing as you were thinking of having him painted."

Lady H huffed and pursed her lips. "This is not the traditional pose for a thoroughbred painting. We wanted him in his stall, turning his head, with . . ."

"Good grief, Marianne, don't you recognize originality when you see it? This is marvellous! Marvellous! Who is this chap? How much does he want?"

"Our mutual friend said to tell you . . . in case you might be interested, that is . . . to offer the artist what *you* think it's worth."

"Good lord."

"Oh give him fifty pounds, Hugh, if you *must* have it."

"Not the budget we had in mind," he chuckled. He frowned, took off his glasses and rubbed his forehead.

Lady H rolled her eyes.

He turned to his wife. "I agree we shouldn't go overboard," he said carefully. "He's obviously unknown. But darling, we can do better than insult him with fifty quid."

The exasperated Marianne knew she had lost the argument. "Well don't be long, darling," she countered sharply. "Dinner in twenty." Glaring at Travis, she swept out of the room.

Both men stared after her, preoccupied. Lord H, like a terrier with a rabbit, was not to be deterred. "Come on, Travis, who is this chap?"

"No idea, milord. Won't give out his name."

"Come, come. Your mutual friend must know."

Travis spread his hands wordlessly, compressed his lips and raised his eyebrows.

"Hmm." He scratched his ear. "The fellow's not in jail, is he? Or anything?"

"No, milord. That I *do* know." *Might do him good, though.*

"Humph." There was a pause. "Well, we'll have to work out something. I don't claim to know much about art. Inherited this lot." He nodded at a gloomy portrait over the staircase. "My youngest does, though. I dare say he'd know whether this fellow is worth collecting."

* * *

May went off two days later to meet relatives over from Australia. She was showing them the sights of London. "Well," she corrected herself, "going round" with them, anyway. Catching up with family news down under." It was a prospect she had been looking forward to all summer.

She sat, now, with her shoes off, rubbing her aching feet. They had spent the morning tramping round the Houses of Parliament, where, in two hours, there had been nowhere at any point to sit down. May, her nephews Martin and Gerry, nieces Emma and Diane, twelve-year old Harry and teens Joanne and Liam, were all sitting in a tired but cheery little group in a café near Broadcasting House. They were booked on a tour of the BBC that afternoon.

Over the juice bar, the lunchtime TV news burbled on in the background. The economy was rallying, there had been a shooting in Hackney, the U.S. president was having trouble again with Congress.

The young contingent was comparing photos they had taken the day before in Trafalgar Square. The adults were still eating. "My feet are blasted," said Emma loudly, making a face and eliciting sympathy from the next table.

"Ar, you'll live," grinned her husband as he loaded up a forkful of battered fish. "Can't let a little thing like feet upset you that easy. This is war! Can't let you Poms be one up . . ." He looked around at the nearest tables, grinning amiably. He turned to Gerry and Diane. "I reckon we could . . ."

"Wasn't that great," chortled Liam, "when that bobby said . . ."

"It's rude to interrupt," shouted Harry.

Joanne scowled at him. "Stop shouting!" It was the third time that day.

"Well, it is," retorted Harry, irrepressible as ever. "Mum said so. You should . . ."

"Ssshhh!" May had gone suddenly rigid."Are we making too much noise, Auntie May?" Us Aussies are a bit loud, I kno . . ."

"Ssshhh!" She held up her hand for quiet, still grasping her fork. The newscaster was delivering a human interest story at the end of the news. Puzzled, they all looked up at the screen.

". . . as of yesterday!" said the newscaster. "Shock headlines appeared in The Sun and The Times this morning. It seems that the artist Porter "Pogy" Spears, who came forward as the painter of the now famous "Horse by the Canal", has been exposed as a fraud. His ex-girlfriend, who, according to The Sun, dumped him following discovery that he had been sleeping with her sister, and according to The Times, broke her engagement because she wanted to devote more time to her studies, said that he had hit on the idea to generate some cash to top up his student loan and to impress his father, Professor Gareth Spears, who thought an art qualification was a waste of time."

May's shoulders began to shake.

"Neither father nor son has been available for comment. However, Professor Spears this morning released a statement saying that his son was off to Uganda to do voluntary work digging wells."

She laughed aloud.

"Pogy Spears," the announcer went on--and here a picture of Pogy filled the screen behind him--"has made a tidy sum giving interviews and appearing on chat shows."

The screen changed to show the canal horse picture. "This poses, once again, the question: Who is the real artist of the "Horse by the Canal"?" The picture was superseded by a gigantic question mark. "So far, no one has come forward. Will he reveal his identity now? (Of course it might be a she.) Or are more people going to claim to be Spartacus?"

May gave a yell of jubilation and punched the air with her fork.

"Ssshhh!" said Harry.

*   *   *

On Wednesday evening, Henry Pierce arrived at the houseboat as he had promised. He brought an assistant and a great deal of tape, cardboard and bubble wrap. The assistant, a beanpole of a young man called Monty, set to work wrapping and packing Robert's paintings with the greatest of care. Pierce was disappointed that Rita had decided to keep two of the best landscapes and an amusing portrait of a border collie baffling a flock of sheep, which he had always fancied himself. But he knew not to push his luck. His buyers had been waiting a long time to acquire Robert's work.

He said with gusto: "I see you've got a new room, Rita." The remark seemed to puzzle her for a moment. He indicated the paintings, neatly stacked at one end of the living room, where Monty, whistling under his breath, was busily packing. He added with misplaced bonhomie: "Must be useful to have the extra space!"

She fought a rush of pain. For a moment, she felt sorry for him. His clumsy attempts to re-establish the rapport she and her husband had once had with him were not succeeding. She forced herself to smile. In a voice as light as she could make it, she added: "Well, it's been a long time."

He nodded. "Probably wise." He patted her hand. "The studio's a reminder, I imagine."

Rita quelled her irritation and decided to take the bull by the horns. "Actually, Mr. Pierce, er, Henry, the studio is still . . . being used . . . A young man I think might have a future in art. He's being a bit secretive, experimenting and all. But my friends and I have seen what he can do. I thought he could put the studio to good use."

Henry Pierce studied her. He wondered fleetingly if Robert's widow might be finding consolation with a toy boy. "Will I have heard of him?"

"No. And he wants to stay anonymous as long as he can." She paused. "We've all had to swear to that."

"Swear?"

A fractional pause. "He's very young."

He waited for her to continue. She didn't. "How young?"

"Sixteen."

Henry Pierce would have laughed if it had been anyone but Rita. "And this er, promising young artist, does he go to school, have parents, friends? Are you going to encourage him to go to art school?"

"No . . . well, yes, . . . no. Perhaps, when he's ready, you might like to have a look at his work, give him your professional opinion?" She rushed on. "I'd like to tell you about him, Henry, when you've time. It's a bit hard to explain."

"I'm intrigued." He was doing his best to keep the irony in check. "Why don't you show me his work now? I mean, I *am* here."

Rita heard the subtext: *No need to bother telling me the boy's history if his so-called "art" is a load of tripe.* She felt a brief moment of panic. What *was* Finn doing in there? But she thought of the horse by the canal, the painting up at the Hall, May's pencil portrait and trusted her instincts.

They began loading everything into the van. Rita went outside to watch. She wanted to say her own quiet farewell. The final link was severing.

Finn arrived, as she knew he would. It had been a vague idea to try and get them together, although she hadn't meticulously planned it. She knew it was probably too soon. But it wouldn't hurt Finn to make Pierce's acquaintance. She called out to catch him before he crossed the gangplank. He came over, noting the flurry of activity around the agent's van. He looked at her quizzically. "It's all right, Finn, Mr Pierce is Robert's agent. He's just collecting the rest of my husband's work." She stared up at the western sky, where the blue was fading into streamers of yellow and orange. It seemed oddly appropriate. She said simply: "It was time."

Pierce walked over and joined them. He stared at Finn. The boy looked wary. Pierce turned to Rita, eyebrows raised.

"Henry, this is Finn. Finn, Henry Pierce." They looked at each other dubiously and nodded.

Finn said at once: "I'd better go." Rita opened her mouth to say something, but he added abruptly: "Sorry to interrupt," nodded again at Pierce, turned and walked off. But Pierce noted he did not go back the way he had come. He headed towards the studio picture window.

"That's him, isn't it?"

Rita hesitated, held his gaze. "Let me talk to him a minute, Henry. Please stay a few minutes. Some tea? A drink?"

He sighed. *Oh well, perhaps.* He was, despite everything, curious, while still being all too aware that many cats were killed that way. He called to Monty to wait for him in the van. Monty reached happily for his smartphone. Pierce followed Rita back into the houseboat.

"Scotch and soda on the rocks, wasn't it?" Pierce looked somewhat mollified. "Sit down, Henry, relax." She poured him a generous drink, raised her hands, palms forward, to signify he should wait and hurried off to the studio.

She knocked. No answer. "Finn?" She knocked again. "Please, open the door. It's only me." Moments went by. "Finn!" He opened the door warily. She saw he had dispensed with the sheet and had bought himself a proper overall.

She was not going to beat about the bush. She had artist and agent in the same house and she was not about to lose the advantage. "I know you didn't want to show us anything you've been doing, and we've respected that. But," she said gently, "I would, please, like you to do one thing for me now." She gave no hint of him owing her, by either inflection or look. But he knew she could have. He didn't want to upset her, but he felt a rising panic.

"Henry wants to see your work, Finn. If he likes it, he can help you a lot. Are you going to move to the next stage? The painting for the Hall was the first. They loved it. You've made some money. Don't go and shoot yourself in the foot. Let him see what you've done so far." She added quietly: "I'd like to see it, too."

He hovered in the doorway, a picture of indecision. "What if he *doesn't* like it? At all? Hates it? What if *you* don't . . ?"

"He will," said Rita, with more confidence than she felt. "And so will I. He'll have to agree to respect your privacy . . ." She saw his face change. ". . . your *anonymity*," she amended hastily. "We'll ask him to give us his word, swear, of course." Finn's expression suggested he was far from convinced. "He's an honest man. That's partly why he and Robert had such a good relationship. He's always been trustworthy, always treated us fairly."

He ran his hand through his hair and seemed to be looking for a way of escape.

She played her master card. "Come on, Finn! I never took you for a coward."

*   *   *

Henry Pierce strolled into the studio, striving, for Rita's sake, not to let derision show on his face. *Whatever I find!*

What he found was a large, full-length portrait of Rita, in green—the dress she had been wearing on the day Finn sketched her watering plants on the veranda. He had set up his two easels one behind the other to face the visitors. Rita's picture was on the first. She was not watering plants. Her body was half turned towards a huge swan swaying, wings spread, at her feet. It was watching her face devotedly, its beak pointing up as if it were about to address her or give her a kiss. But Rita was not looking at Charlie. She had turned her head suddenly, with a surprised laugh, to the artist, who had evidently just said something amusing. He had caught the precise moment. The impression of movement, of humour danced through the painting. It radiated spontaneity.

Rita herself was thunderstruck. *He was only sketching me for a few minutes!* Pierce was equally taken aback. His eyes were riveted, his mouth forming a perfectly rounded 'o'. Rita moved back to where Finn stood quietly near the door, as if afraid he might need to make a quick exit. He couldn't look at her. Her eyes danced. "Oh Finn." He heard the smile in her voice and looked up. "I love it! However did you do it?" She squeezed his arm.

Pierce moved behind the easel to the second painting. Once more, both were astonished. It was May, a May that Rita recognized, but had never imagined before. She stood regally, in an elegant, narrow evening gown he had found in a magazine. Fragile blue silk shimmered beneath the most delicate overlay of lace. A blue chiffon stole barely touched her shoulders. Pierce moved closer. He exhaled loudly. "God almighty!"

He stepped back again to study May's face. He thought he had met this lady before, but could not place her. His appraising eye took in the suggestion of a tiara, picked up May's joie de vivre, her capacity for affection, her ability to be utterly herself. It was all in her decisive but slightly amused expression. The eyes said it all, as did the generous curve of the mouth. She was standing slightly off-centre, one gloved hand resting on the corner of a stone balcony carved in a tracery of leaves. She was bathed in the light of a summer evening, against a backdrop of oaks and beeches.

"Does it have a title?"

Rita didn't know whether he was addressing her, or Finn fidgeting in the background. He muttered something inaudible.

Pierce tried again. "Sorry, er, Finn. I didn't catch that."

"It's called 'Ma'am'."

"That's what they call the Queen," said Pierce, in a slightly shocked voice.

"May's a 'Ma'am' as well. Thought I'd paint her that way."

Rita gave a delighted laugh. "She'll love it."

Pierce turned to look at Finn. "Where in god's name did you learn to paint like this?"

Silence.

Rita came to his rescue. "He didn't."

"What!"

"That's one of the things I wanted to explain, Henry."

A stunned silence followed.

Finn cleared his throat. "There . . . there's another one. I'll get it." He lifted May's picture carefully off the easel and placed it against the wall. He picked up another canvas that had been turned the wrong way, and placed it on the easel.

This one was a painting of Kath and Connor. Pierce stared, open-mouthed.

"This is my sister and her little boy, said Finn. "We're . . . they're Catholic. So . . . that's why I did it this way. Sort of suits her."

No one spoke.

Rita came up behind him and put her hands on his shoulders.

The picture had none of the sophistication of May's portrait, or the electric spontaneity of Rita's. Mother and child were in a sunlit meadow. Kath wore a sapphire-blue head scarf and a matching, short, blue dress. She was smiling gently down at Connor, who lay gurgling and kicking in her lap. The baby, wrapped in a little white blanket, had a garland of daisies around his head. A corner of the blanket had flopped over, revealing a border of tiny, appliqued farm animals.

The composition had a whimsical charm. Kath was dangling one foot in a fast-running stream. The other she had tucked underneath her to help cradle the baby. Part of what might have been a gypsy wagon was just visible at the edge of the painting.

But it was her face that was the focal point of the composition. The deceptively gentle expression was alive with a quiet, mischievous delight. Beneath it, Pierce discerned a contentment too deep for words.

How the hell did he do that? The picture, like its subject matter, exuded ambiguities.

Pierce was still standing with one hand clamped to the top of his head. He let it drop and turned to look at Finn, who had been staring nervously at the floor.

"My god, Rita." Pierce waved his arm around to indicate the pictures, then looked at Finn. "What *have* we got here? First there was Mozart, and now . . . !"

"Swear, Henry!"

"Bugger me!" he yelled.

She laughed. "No, come on."

"Yes, yes! Give you my word of honour, though how long we can . . ." He laughed aloud, marched across to Finn and stuck out his hand. Finn took it gravely.

"How long we can keep you a secret, my dear boy, I do not know."

He caught sight of another picture discreetly turned the wrong way.

"What's that great big canvas over there?" His voice dropped to an excited whisper. "Can we see it?"

Finn was silent for a moment. He looked at Rita. "I'll show it to *you*, Mr Pierce. But Rita isn't to see it. Not yet. 'T isn't finished."

Rita gave an exaggerated shrug and threw up her hands in mock outrage. "We should celebrate. I'll get us some champagne."

There were two bottles in the fridge. Torn between jubilation and remorse, she had gone out and bought them in her lunch hour after May rang to tell her the news about Spears. A fraud! A fraud after all! May had been right all along! Rita had wished the ground would open up. There was no help for it but to face Finn and tell him straight out.

She had tried. He came to the studio door at her second knock, clearly busy and not sure why she was interrupting him. He stood in the doorway wiping a smudge of paint off his cheek with a rag. She forced herself to look him in the face but had to look away almost at once.

"Anything wrong?"

She paused, took a deep breath and spelled it out to him as directly as she could. He stared at the floor, his expression hard to read. He said nothing. She had planned to stop there. But she heard herself stumbling, trying to explain, needing to apologise. Her voice tailed off. He looked up, very still. They stared at each other in silence. "Look," he said simply, "I could . . . I could sort of see where you were coming from. No point getting upset now. I already had my strop."

"He said that?" said May when she came back the next day. "What did he . . . ?

"He said he took an axe and hacked some old furniture and stuff to bits, that they'd put on the community pile for a bonfire and he didn't stop til he'd turned it into matchwood. Oh, and he put his fist through a box of eggs, apparently."

She could barely look at her friend. "Oh May, I'm so sorry. I should have believed you. And what poor Finn must have gone through! I shouldn't have . . ."

May had interrupted the litany of guilt. "Never mind the 'if only's'. This isn't a time to be morbid! This is a time to celebrate!" She flung her arms in the air. "Where's that champagne? Is Finn here?" Rita nodded. "Why don't you fetch him? Accept no excuses." She touched Rita's arm. "Don't worry. We'll save some for Travis."

"It'll probably choke him," said Rita. But she smiled.

Rita stood now in her kitchen and almost hugged herself with satisfaction. Could it have turned out any better? Finn had an agent, a dependable one. Henry had a new client, a mysterious boy prodigy, alias Spartacus. (Within hours of the broadcast, the name had stuck.) *Ha! What could be more normal?* She wrestled with the last bottle of champagne. There was a loud pop, but she was careful. Not a drop fizzed out. She poured herself a preliminary glass and quietly wished them a satisfying--and profitable--partnership. *May will be ecstatic.* She paused, smiled gently. *Robert would have been pretty entertained, too.*

*   *   *

Outside the gallery a spanking new banner hung above the entrance:

"IN AT THE BEGINNING"
A Special Exhibition.

August 25th to September 10th

Inside, next to the visitors' desk, was a notice on a wooden stand:

This is a debut exhibition.

The pictures you are about to see are the work of a new artist who wishes for the moment to remain anonymous.

He is entirely self-taught.

We hope you enjoy it.

(No photographs allowed, except by registered members of the press.)

Displayed on the desk were some loose leaves announcing that the pictures in the Special Exhibition were not, at the moment, for sale. "However, prints will be available shortly. Please write your details on the sheet provided if you would like to receive further information about ordering."

Finn took Kath and Declan to the exhibition the day before the official opening. Henry had pointed out that as fish out of water they would soon invite interrogation by the curious and Finn's cover would be blown. They had already been introduced to Rita and May. But no matter how forewarned they were, they were bound to draw attention by their reaction when they saw their pictures. And in any case, the one of Kath and Connor would give the game away on the spot.

Finn himself had more faith in their reliability and had vigorously argued the point. He also pointed out that Kath often changed her appearance in the name of fashion, so it was hardly a stumbling block.

They had reached an impasse when Kath herself suggested that perhaps they could just come earlier, with Finn. She didn't want to leave the baby behind and it wasn't the sort of event where a baby would be welcome. "I don't think we'd be comfortable with all those arty people, I do not," was Declan's comment.

Henry had heaved a sigh of relief.

The notice and desk fliers alone overwhelmed them even before they saw the paintings. Finn left them to it and sat jiggling Connor on his knee. He felt as nervous as a girl before her first dance. What would they think?

His sister and brother-in-law were flabbergasted.

*   *   *

On the evening of the official opening the gallery was already heaving after twenty minutes. Finn watched the expressions of the guests Henry had invited as they strolled around with their glasses of champagne and stared at his work. He was posing as an inquisitive cleaner who was trying to stay out of sight and do his job in other parts of the gallery, while popping his head round a pillar occasionally to gawp. He wore an overall, a baseball cap on backwards with his hair tucked out of sight, and carried a bucket and mop for good measure. He attracted a number of frowns for making himself visible. There were mutterings to Henry.

"Cheeky beggar!" Henry apologised. "I'll deal with him at once." A glare and raised eyebrow were enough to encourage Finn to make himself scarce for a while. They were usually followed by a wink.

About to duck out a side door, he saw, with savage delight, that one of the new arrivals was Miss Johnson, the school art teacher. She was, after all, a member of the county Fine Art Society. As she came up the steps, he accidentally put himself in her way. She didn't recognize him for a moment, then looked him up and down contemptuously. He pretended surprise and embarrassment. "Yes, I thought that's about where you'd end up," she sniffed. "Still, I suppose we should be grateful you've bothered to get a job at all." She swept past and entered the gallery. *Hah!* He would have punched the air if he hadn't been holding a bucket. He would have to ask Henry what she thought.

May had loaned her pencil drawing for the exhibition, and Finn had enhanced it with delicate touches of pastel. Henry framed it. The drawing of Connor, on loan from Kath and Declan, received similar treatment. Both pictures were untitled and only signed with his initials on the back. May had nagged him to death to make sure he claimed them as his own in some fashion.

It was the same story with the painting of Kath and Connor and the one of Rita. There was much deliberation about them. "That's Leda and the swan," proclaimed an astute-looking man who might have been a university professor. "Our mystery artist is obviously well acquainted with the classics." There were a few murmurs of agreement. A high-end antiques dealer with a penchant for French literature instantly disagreed. "It's a reference to Proust."

A little group of well-off art fanciers, however, arrived at a different conclusion. "Isn't that . . . good gracious, isn't that Rita Dean?" said Sadie.

"Dean? *Robert* Dean's widow?" said Ralph.

They stared in silence.

Their friend Penelope slowly nodded. "You know, I . . ." She paused, then burst out excitedly: "I think you're right!" There were murmurs of agreement from the others.

"Well," said Paul, her executive husband, "*she* knows this artist fellow, doesn't she? Mystery solved! Must be a friend of her husband's."

Ralph chuckled. "She'll have to spill the beans sooner or later, won't she?"

A reporter, briefed to write up the exhibition for the most cultural of the county magazines, just missed overhearing as they moved away. He stopped to lean against a pillar and make notes on his ipad. He had already been round taking pictures. He wanted to get everything done fast and then wangle a second glass of bubbly.

The painting of Flying Dutchman was also attracting considerable comment. Leicestershire is a horsey county. Opinions were divided. Most people seemed unashamedly enthusiastic. A few were displeased by the painting's unconventionality. One or two promptly revised their opinion when they saw the painting was on loan courtesy of Lord and Lady H.

May nudged Rita and whispered: "Wait til they see the one of Kath and Connor."

The two women mingled without comment. Rita wore a business suit, glasses and a blonde wig in a stylish bob. May had decided to go bohemian. Her hair was hidden under a mannish hat, teemed with horn-rimmed spectacles, an old, "flower child" top, tatty jeans and wellingtons. She attracted the occasional sniff of distaste, but for the most part both she and Rita were able to stroll about in peace.

Travis was busy up at the stables, and as he didn't think Lord H, who couldn't come until the next day, would relish him tagging along, said he'd stick his head round the door later on.

May had been too moved by Finn's homage to stand and gaze at his painting of her. She had done her gazing beforehand. But she did dig Rita in the ribs when they heard a well-known sponsor of the arts remark, as he studied the painting: "Dammit if she doesn't make me want to sweep her a bow." The young fashionista on his arm added, with cloying sweetness, that it was *lovely* to see the elegance of an older woman appreciated for a change. May wondered if the girl would have the same opinion if she could see her now. She giggled.

They walked into the next room, taut with excitement. Finn had promised they would only get to see the new painting when it was put on show. (To which Travis remarked that the kid had a flair for drama.) May and Rita gazed at the immense oil painting, displayed all by itself on a pristine white wall.

The caption read: BALLINASLOE HORSE FAIR (Oil on canvas).

Finn had created an extraordinarily intricate composition of lively, socialising gypsies and horses from what he recalled of Irish horse fairs. Boys trotted by, bareback, on piebald ponies. Dainty thoroughbreds were being led up and down, showing their paces for prospective buyers, whose bartering faces were full of bonhomie and sly calculation. An organized fist fight had attracted a little crowd. There was Da, winning his bout and Reese, waving his arms in excitement. Ma sat in a wagon, looking on and smiling to herself. To the right of the painting, in the foreground, sat a woman in profile, calmly watching the proceedings. She wore a blue dress and resembled Rita to the life. Her expression conveyed a sweet serenity. Rita was entranced. A stray dog was barking at no one in particular. "That's Finn," said Rita, pointing. May giggled. "And look at you!" She pointed. May stared. A woman stood to the left of the picture, in the middle ground. She was wearing a soft, cream dress and carried the extravagant hat May had been wearing when Finn first met her. She was out of place, yet a focal point crucial to the flow of the painting. Her face was keenly alive as she pointed with delight at a trotting race in the background.

Rita gave a little gasp. She nudged May and nodded. May followed her eyes. Scrawled in the bottom, right-hand corner of the picture was the letter S and a tiny gladiator's sword.

* * *

Of course, it wasn't long before somebody saw the connection with the "Horse by the Canal". Within days, "Ballinasloe Horse Fair" went viral. Finn's other pictures followed. "Spartacus has been busy!" was a feature in the magazine section of The Mail on Sunday.

He had stood distractedly in the studio remembering the impact as his pictures had exploded over the internet. "Oh, let YouTube do its worst," May said, attempting a hearty tone. But she had looked more anxious than he had ever seen her.

He said nothing, biting his lip and staring into space. Then he scoffed dismissively. "Daft idiots." May's frown deepened. He held her gaze. Then, slowly, faintly, he smiled.

She saw with sudden, overwhelming relief that his equilibrium was not going to be shaken. "You just . . . just do whatever *you* want to do," she burst out.

He grinned at her. Then he threw his head back and laughed aloud. She joined in. He swept her a bow, "Ma'am," and raised his palm. They high-fived.

*   *   *

Two more people claimed to be Spartacus. A girl, who did it as a hoax to give herself fifteen minutes of fame. And a middle-aged man who lived with his mother and, so far as anyone knew, had never picked up an artist's brush in his life. His elderly mother stood by his claim. "If Clarence says he's Spartacle, I believe him. My son has always been a dark horse. But brilliant," she added.

A flurry of reporters tracked the man down and subjected him and his mother to the camera flashes and relentless attempts at interrogation more suitable to crime drama. They desisted only when, asked what he was going to paint next, Clarence said, with airy confusion: "Er . . . Mum's bedroom . . . er . . . what?"

*   *   *

Right now, alone in the studio, Finn was too busy to care about the world's opinion, or even Miss Johnson's, which had apparently been ecstatic. He selected a brush and was immediately absorbed in his new canvas. Unlike Wandering Aengus, he knew he had at last cornered his own elusive, glimmering goal. He was utterly happy.

ABOUT THE AUTHOR

I'm not quite sure how to describe myself, as I've been a bit of a Jack of all Trades. A career as a child model was cut short when I fell off the catwalk at the age of five. An omen, no doubt, as I've been horribly prone to accidents ever since. These include a narrow escape from a stampeding herd of cattle, a near-miss incident on a jumbo jet, jumping from a bolting horse seconds before it charged under a signpost, falling downstairs carrying a tray of glasses, being on a transatlantic flight when an engine burst into flames (right next to my window), getting stuck under a ladder at the bottom of a swimming pool, falling into the river as I was supposed to be skipping from a boat onto the quay, and being mugged in a New York lift---which left me highly concussed, and probably explains a lot.

Exciting jobs include tour guiding, putting the shine on Avon lipsticks, promoting cubic zirconia jewellery and picking mushrooms. My career as a waitress lasted a week after I dropped profiteroles in a customer's lap.

But it hasn't all been doom and gloom. There have been high points, particularly dog-sledding by lantern light in Alaska and riding a dolphin (elsewhere, obviously). I also attended the mushers' banquet before the start of the great Alaskan Iditarod. To a lesser degree, going to a Star Trek convention right after attending a dreary modern languages conference the week before, at the same venue, takes a bit of beating.

On the more responsible side, I did work for NASA for a short time (saw the "blue book", met astronauts), right after a graduate stint at Columbia University in New York. I then worked as a professional translator for American corporations and, occasionally, the law courts. I'm currently an educator and live near Brighton.

I discovered too late in life that I had an operatic voice--well, too late for a professional career, anyway. But drama, opera and musical comedy have figured prominently in my life, and I've appeared in a number of productions (and concerts), as well as directed a few.

The writers' group of five that I have belonged to since it's inception has, dauntingly, already produced C J Sansom and William Shaw, and our honorary member, Lucy Anne Holmes, the daughter of our fourth member, Mike Holmes (no relation to Sherlock). In their shadow, my own "standard works" include a radio play, a collection of 32 humorous dog stories, some poetry, a pilot for a sit-com (with Roz Brody, the fifth member of the group), a lyrical piece in "This England" and most recently, "Spanish Phoenix", a historical drama in four episodes written for TV.

What else? Let's see. I like to paint while listening to thrillers on audio books with my "significant other". Writing songs has been an absorbing revelation. I collect antiques and curios (minimalists are not very comfortable in my home.) I love meeting up with friends, especially where restaurants are involved! I've travelled quite a lot, but still feel most at home in the countryside or going for long walks on the beach with my border collie, Jack--which is the only place I can take him where he can't chase trains or attack double-decker buses.